Gun from the Outside

This Large Print Book carries the
Seal of Approval of N.A.V.H.

GUN FROM THE OUTSIDE

RAY HOGAN

THORNDIKE PRESS

A part of Gale, Cengage Learning

GALE
CENGAGE Learning

Detroit • New York • San Francisco • New Haven, Conn • Waterville, Maine • London

LIBRARY OF CONGRESS CATALOGING-IN-PUBLICATION DATA

Hogan, Ray, 1908–1998.
  Gun from the Outside / by Ray Hogan. — Large Print edition.
    pages cm. — (Thorndike Press Large Print Western)
  ISBN-13: 978-1-4104-5677-9 (hardcover)
  ISBN-10: 1-4104-5677-3 (hardcover)
  1. Fathers and sons—Fiction. 2. Conflict of generations—Fiction. 3. Large
type books. I. Title.
PS3558.O3473O93 2013
813'.54—dc23
                                                        2012047521

Published in 2013 by arrangement with Golden West Literary Agency

Printed in the United States of America
1 2 3 4 5 6 7 17 16 15 14 13

GUN FROM THE OUTSIDE

I

This was Big Bill Krask's town. Dan Wade pulled the roan to a halt on the crest of the ridge and looked down upon the T-shaped collection of buildings and houses. The sun was beginning to lower beyond the hills to the west and he allowed his eyes to travel up the darkening cañon that lay between the twin rows of high, false-fronted structures.

Lights were coming on in the windows of several stores and in most of the homes scattered across the land behind the commercial buildings where the supper hour would be at hand. It would be hot in the kitchens, Dan thought, studying the trickles of smoke snaking upward into the night sky. The day had been a scorcher, but there was no answer to the problem. Women must still feed their men, their families.

It had been eight years since he had left Burnt Springs. It appeared to have grown little in the intervening time. The same signs on the front of the buildings, the same names, the same owners were also in evidence. Yet there had been one change. It had brought him all the way across Texas and half the distance that spanned New Mexico Territory. He thought of that, of the letter folded and tucked away inside his shirt pocket. It had caught up with him in

Abilene and immediately set the wheels of memory and curiosity to turning within his mind.

Dear Friend Dan:
If you can find time to ride by, I'll be much obligated. Find myself in considerable trouble and could sure use your help.

Yours truly,
Wm. Krask, Marshal

Two things in the letter had startled and amazed him — that Big Bill would ever ask anyone for help, and that he had become a lawman. Krask had been, or was, the owner of the vast Double K spread, a magnificent ranch lying deep in the broad, grassy depths of the Cloud River Valley. Undisputable king of that part of the territory, he was wealthy, successful, and never in need of anything or anybody. Why he should become a lawman, a marshal of a town he figuratively owned, was difficult to understand. But Big Bill had been a friend, the first man to give Dan a job when the war was over and jobs were hard to come by. He was a widower, his wife having died soon after their son Little Bill, as he had become known, was born. Krask lived only for his son, building his future, his life, the ranch — everything — about him.

Someday Little Bill would inherit and take over the Double K. He would instantly be the biggest man in the territory, the most important figure in the entire Southwest. Big Bill had great plans for his only son and he never permitted him, or anyone else, to forget it. Little Bill had been about sixteen, Dan recalled, when he had decided to quit the Double K and ride on: a big, good-looking boy, the image of his father but inclined to wildness and with a broad streak of reckless irresponsibility running through his nature. Big Bill spent a considerable amount of time and money getting him out of scrapes. And always the cattleman had laughed it off, brushed it aside as a normal and natural thing for a high-spirited boy.

Little Bill had never become involved in anything serious. Generally it was nothing more than a combination of too much freedom, an over-supply of money resulting in a tremendous amount of mischief. There was never a time, so far as Dan knew, when anyone was maliciously injured. But apparently something had finally happened. Little Bill had gotten himself into a pocket so critical that the elder Krask had felt the need for help. This did not explain the lawman angle, however. Why would Big Bill, important, wealthy, a man more likely to be governor of the territory, assume the thankless task of a town marshal?

Dan Wade stirred impatiently. He removed his hat, ran a hand through his thick shock of light brown hair. He disliked unanswered questions, unsolved problems. It disturbed him when he could not find the solutions.

A gunshot sounded in the settlement, hollow and distant as it echoed through the lush, low hills and across the frothy green swales. He stiffened, his wide shoulders silhouetted against the dark sky, head thrust forward. He probed the shadowy street and buildings with sharp, pale eyes, but the distance was too great, the night too near. He could make out nothing.

He reached down, touched the heavy and worn Colt .44 hanging at his hip. His long fingers lifted it slightly in its oiled holster, let it fall again into place. What lay ahead in Burnt Springs was uncertain. Soon he would know.

He pressed the roan gelding gently with his spurs, starting him down the slope. The horse was tired. It had been a long, sweltering ride from Mesilla but he responded instantly, taking the steep trail of the grade with careful, sure-footed steps.

They reached the bottom, swung

into the ankle-deep dust of the road that led on to El Paso, Mexico, and points farther south. Dan remembered it well. It had been the route he had followed that day when the urge to move on had eventually overwhelmed him. It seemed like a long, long time ago.

He came into town, his glance flipping from side to side as he approached the end of the street. There had been no more gunshots. He could hear men yelling, laughing, the faint strains of piano music. Somewhere beyond the Rainbow Saloon and Dance Hall, which sprawled at the opposite end of the settlement on the one cross street, thus forming a dead end, the sudden hammering of hoofs told of a horse breaking away and into a hard, quick run.

To his immediate left the first building, which had once housed a small, rag-tag saloon, was vacant. Next to it Joe Kingsford's hardware store was still doing business, its windows piled high with washtubs, buckets, brooms, and the like. Then came a ladies' dress and millinery shop, owned, Dan recalled, by prim and prudish Miss Agatha Hillard. A doctor and a lawyer maintained offices in the succeeding building, all of which were dark.

Beyond the professional men's quarters and in direct sequence was a barbershop, another small saloon, a second-rate hotel called the Star of Texas, and then the largest general store in the area, one belonging to Tom Hotchkiss. Burnt Springs' one cross street intersected there, brought an end to the line of structures. On the opposite side there came first a small store of some sort, groceries and meats it appeared to Dan. There was no sign on the dusty window or above the door and he could not be sure. A clothing store was beside it, followed by the marshal's office and jail, the Chicago Café, Abner Dawson's Cattleman's Bank, and the tall, two-storied bulk of the Great Western Hotel.

Wade halted the roan in front of Kingsford's, momentarily undecided whether to go first to the marshal's office, or to the Great Western and procure a room. There were few people on the street and those were down near the Rainbow. Glancing at them, he noted that a man named Garvey still operated the stable that lay directly to the east of the saloon. He could not tell who occupied the store buildings at its opposite shoulder. There had been a printer there formerly, a small, wizened man who endeavored, without much success, to produce a weekly newspaper.

There was a light in the marshal's office. The Chicago Café also was open for business. The saloon next to the Texas Star was bright but all the remaining buildings were dark except, of course, the Great Western Hotel and the Rainbow, which blazed with lamps and resounded with the racket created by its boisterous patrons.

He decided he would go first to the hotel, to its stable in the rear. The roan deserved a stall along with the care and rest that went with it. And he could use a bit of freshening up himself. Another thirty minutes would make little difference.

He put the gelding into motion, resumed his slow progress down the dark avenue, his eyes again roving the faces of the structures, probing the black passageways that lay between. He looked carefully at the marshal's office, endeavored to see behind its dusty window. There was no one sitting at the desk. Likely Big Bill was having his supper at that hour.

He drew abreast the Chicago Café. He could use a good meal himself, particularly some strong, black coffee. It had been early morning since he had eaten. After he cleaned up, he would pay a call on the café. There would be ample time. Down in front of the Rainbow a man shouted, a woman laughed in a high-pitched, almost hysterical way. He swung his attention to that point. Somewhere back off among the houses a church bell tolled the faithful to prayer meeting and a dog barked in a slow, measured beat.

It was the same — yet there was change. Dan Wade could feel it in the hot, breathless air, in the silence, in the deserted street. Burnt Springs was a trouble town. He had ridden into too many not to recognize the signs. That apparently was the reason. He stiffened on the saddle, small stabs of warning jabbing suddenly at his consciousness. He became aware of two shadows sliding from the darkness along the south wall of the Texas Star. He drew up slowly, his hand easing toward the pistol at his hip. A voice, arrogant with whiskey, sliced through the night.

"Just where you think you're goin', mister?"

II

A third man, standing unseen a few paces to the side, spoke up: "Don't go reachin' for that iron! Could be right unhealthy."

Dan settled back on his saddle. Tension and a bright flow of anger simmered through him but he held his peace, keeping himself in check. He waited out the moments in dead silence. He watched the men move in nearer, saw the dull glitter of dim lamplight seeping through the streaky glass of the Texas Star's window, as it touched the gun in the speaker's hand. One of the trio swaggered to the head of the gelding; the other two ranged up on either side.

Wade said: "What's this all about?"

The man in front of him cocked his head to one side. He was a squat, husky individual and wore his broad-brimmed hat well back. Even in the poor light his hair showed brick red.

"Like I said before, where you think you're goin'?"

"Happens to be my business but I was headed for the hotel. You got objections?"

The rider on the right laughed. "You hear that, Cully?" he said, speaking to the redhead. "He's wantin' to know do we have objections."

Cully adjusted the position of his headgear. "Might just say we do, seein' as how we own this town. You

21

lookin' for somebody special?"

Wade stirred. He was a man with a low boiling point and the moment was dangerously near. "Also my business," he replied coolly.

The redhead spat. "Maybe it's mine, too. Reckon you'd better climb down off that horse."

Dan stared at the man. He made no effort to comply, simply remained motionless.

"You heard him," the rider to his left said. "Get off that saddle quick unless you want me to yank you off!"

"Never mind, Carl," Cully murmured, drawing his pistol. The hammer clicked loudly as he drew it back. "Looks like he's the wise kind. It's goin' to take a mite of persuadin'."

Wade glanced at the leveled revolver in the redhead's hand, shifted his eyes to that held by the other man. He looked toward the marshal's office. There was no sign of Krask yet. A sudden worry flooded into his mind. Perhaps this was why Big Bill had sent for him — to help wrest the town from men such as these — and he had arrived too late.

"You gettin' down?" Cully's hard, pressing question drove into his thoughts.

Wade shrugged. It would be wise to play out the hand, at least until he knew what it was all about. "Sure, why not?"

"Now that's bein' co-operative," the cowboy to his left said. "Just move away from that horse. And keep your hands up around your ears."

Dan felt the solid ground under his feet. He took a short step toward

Cully.

"Pull his iron, Levi," the redhead said. "Don't want him gettin' no ideas."

Wade was aware of a lessening of weight on his hip as the gun was drawn from its holster, tossed off to one side. He squared himself as Cully put away his own weapon, stepped closer.

"Now we'll do that talkin', mister. What's your name?"

A fresh burst of yelling broke out near the Rainbow. A fight had begun and the hot, night air was suddenly filled with shouts and cursing. The redhead did not turn to look but gazed steadily at Dan.

"Means nothing to you," Wade said. "I could tell you it was Jones and you'd never know the difference."

"He sure is a cute one, ain't he, Cully?" Levi exclaimed. "Maybe I ought to teach him some manners."

The redhead waved him back. "Time enough for that when I'm done talkin'. Ross wants to know all about anybody that rides in. You, Mister Jones" — he added, facing Dan again — "where you headed for besides the hotel?"

"Maybe no place . . . and maybe for some other town where people don't get so nosy."

Cully shook his head slowly. "Levi, I'm thinkin' you're right. This jasper could use a lesson or two. Then he ought to be ready to talk."

Wade felt Levi crowd in on him from behind, saw the man's hand reach for his wrist. Anger roared through him, exploded. He spun fast, caught the cowboy by the arm. Using all his strength, he whipped Levi about, released his grip, sent him crashing into Cully.

Carl yelled in startled surprise as the two men collided, went down into the dust in a tangle of squirming bodies. Wade sprang, was upon him before he could draw his gun. He locked his arms about the smaller man, pinned his hands to his sides. He leaned forward, threw Carl off balance, and then rushed him head-on into the solid, unyielding wall of the Texas Star.

Breath left the cowboy's lungs in a strangled gasp. He went limp in Dan's arms and sank to the ground. Wade whirled. Levi and Cully were scrambling to their feet. He lunged across the intervening space that separated him from them. Levi grabbed frantically for his pistol. Dan's rock-hard fist swung wide, caught him flush on the jaw. It lifted the rider off the ground and laid him flat in the dust.

Cully was on his hands and knees searching about for his weapon that had fallen when Levi had crashed into him. Wade caught the glitter of it, half buried in the loose dirt. He kicked it aside, crossed quickly to where his own gun had been tossed, and scooped it up. He turned to face the redhead. His body still trembled from the violence of his anger and he was sucking deeply for wind. He watched Cully get to his feet.

"Any more questions you want to ask?" he demanded in a low, savage voice.

Cully stared at him. He was plastered with dust and a smear of blood marked the corner of his mouth. "Go to hell," he muttered, pure hatred seething through the words. He pivoted, started off down the street.

"Not so fast!" Wade's voice was like a crackling whip.

The redhead paused, came slowly around. "Yeah?"

"You're forgetting a couple of things . . . your friends there. Take them along."

Cully glanced at Levi. The rider was sitting up, rubbing his jaw painfully. Carl still lay near the saloon. Cully walked to his side, nudged him roughly with the toe of his boot. "Come on, let's go," he said.

Carl stirred to a sitting position. He looked around dazedly. The redhead reached down, took his hand, and pulled him to his feet. Carl focused his eyes on Wade. He swore feelingly.

"That damn' drifter. . . ."

Cully said: "Forget it. Let's go get a drink."

Levi was upright, legs spread, shoulders hunched forward. "I ain't about to . . . not until I've worked this jasper over good."

"And him standin' there with a gun in his hand?" Cully said scornfully. "You help yourself. I'll pick me another time."

Levi relaxed. After a moment he moved over and joined his two friends. "Sure. Always another day."

"Now is as good a time as any," Wade said.

The redhead shrugged. "I'll do the choosin'. Don't be forgettin' that."

"I'll be looking forward to it," Dan said, and watched the three men shamble off down the street for the Rainbow.

He turned to the roan, noted he was almost directly in front of the marshal's office. He gave that a moment's thought, and then led the weary horse to the hitch rack that fronted the building. That no one was inside the lawman's office was evident; the fracas with the three cowpunchers would have brought Krask, or his deputy, into the open, that was certain.

He decided he would leave a note, let the lawman know he had arrived and was at the hotel. It would be just as well and a deal more comfortable to wait in his room. Besides, he felt the need to wash up, to stretch his body across a bed for a few minutes.

He pushed open the door of the office and stepped inside. The room was close with stifling heat, only dimly lit by a single lamp that had been turned low. He walked to the battered desk, twisted the flame higher. He found a sheet of yellowed paper, and procured a snub of pencil from his own pocket. At that exact moment he heard a groan.

He straightened up, senses suddenly alert. The sound had come from the adjoining room, from one of the cells that apparently lay behind a partition. It could be a prisoner, he reasoned, some cowboy who had gotten into a scrap or drunk too much and had been locked inside the cage until he got over it. But Dan Wade's mind refused to accept the explanation.

He thrust the pencil back into his pocket, moved toward the open door that led to the rear of the building. It was dark in the narrow corridor where he found himself and he paused to strike a match. He held it above his head in order better to see. There were two cells and both their doors were open. On a cot in the first a man lay, face down.

Wade stepped inside. The match went out abruptly, scorching his fingers. He swore softly, struck another. Holding it in his left hand, he rolled the man on the cot to his back. There was the sharp glint of metal on his breast as the feeble light reflected against something metallic. Dan bent forward for a better look. It was the five-pointed star of a town marshal. He drew back as the tiny flame again died. Someone had knocked the lawman unconscious and thrown him into his own jail! But the figure on the cot didn't look like Big Bill. Still, in a way. . . .

He fired a third match, again leaned down, this time holding the light nearer the man's face. A gasp of surprise escaped Dan Wade's lips. It was a Krask, all right, but not the one he had expected. The marshal of Burnt Springs was Little Bill.

III

Wade wheeled swiftly, returned to the office. He dipped a cupful of water from the bucket that stood in a corner of the room. Taking also the lamp, he hurried back to the cell.

Finding no cloth of any sort available, he sloshed a quantity of the liquid onto Little Bill's face.

The young lawman stirred. Wade stepped back, placing the lamp on a table at the end of the cot. He looked more closely at Little Bill. There was no blood on him, no evidence of a fight. Apparently he had been hit from behind. After a moment he struggled to a sitting position. His hand went to the back of his head, probing gingerly. Abruptly he stiffened, as though realizing something. He glanced about, brought his eyes to a halt on Wade.

"Who are you . . . ?" he began, and stopped. A wry grin crossed his face. "Dan!" he exclaimed, reaching out his hand. "Sure glad to see you!"

Wade closed the lawman's fingers

in his own. "Looks like I got here a little late."

Krask frowned. "You mean finding me here like this? Not the first time. It's Pa's idea of a joke."

"Big Bill . . . he hit you over the head and threw you in here?"

"Some of his boys did. Happened twice before."

Dan shook his head, perplexed. "I don't think I understand," he said slowly. "When I got the letter, I figured it was Big Bill who'd sent it. Now I find it was you and that your Pa's doing all the hell raising."

"Long story," the lawman said, rising to his feet. "Let's go up front where we can sit down. I'll try to explain."

He started for the door, staggered slightly. Dan caught him by the arm, steadied him. "You sure you're not bad hurt?"

Young Krask nodded. "I'm all right. Takes me a few minutes to get my legs back under me."

Wade picked up the lamp and led the way back to the office. Little Bill, now a man well over six feet, sank into his swivel chair. Dan dragged another up to the desk. He glanced at the young lawman. He had changed considerably since he had last seen him. The wildness was gone from his dark eyes and he had filled out to some extent. He was every bit as large as his father, and just as dark and good-looking — handsome, Dan guessed he could be termed. And he had that same stubborn set to his chin that distinguished Big Bill.

"Thought you'd be running the

Double K by now," he said, opening the conversation. "Surprises me no end seeing you wearing a star."

"Cause of all the trouble," Little Bill replied, drawing tobacco and papers from the top drawer of the desk. He offered them to Wade who shook his head. He began to roll a smoke for himself. "Pa was set on me taking over."

"I remember, he had big plans for you."

"I know, but I never liked ranching. Had some ideas of my own. Pa had my life all worked out for me, the way he wanted it. I couldn't see it."

It had been Big Bill's dream, Dan knew. It was all the cattleman had lived for. Everything he did was for his son who one day would assume command of the huge Double K and carry on the Krask tradition. "Reckon that was a big disappointment to him."

Little Bill completed his cigarette, thrust the slim brown cylinder of tobacco between his lips. "More than that," he said ruefully. "Seems more like it unhinged his mind, the way he began acting."

There was a sudden drumming of horse's hoofs down the street in the direction of the Rainbow. Little Bill rose to his feet, walked to the door, and glanced out. "They're leaving," he said, more to himself than to Dan. "Guess the town can get some sleep now."

He returned to his chair, leaned back wearily. "Last time you saw me, I expect I was one of the worst mavericks you ever came across."

"For a fact," Wade said honestly.

"Couldn't make myself settle down. Didn't like cattle raising and did about everything I could to keep from it. Did a pretty fair job of dodging it, too, I guess. There's hardly a jail in the territory and in West Texas that I haven't spent at least one night in. But Pa always came along and got me out. Then one day I woke up. I met a girl, first one that I ever wanted to marry. Pa was crowding me hard to cut out the foolishness and take over the ranch about that time and all of a sudden I knew I had to make up my mind about things. I screwed up enough guts to tell him ranching wasn't for me, and that I was going to get married and shove off on my own. Saying one to him was bad enough, but hitting him with both really fired him off. He raved for days about it."

"He didn't like this girl you wanted to marry?"

Little Bill shook his head. "He didn't even know Hannah, never had seen her. She lived up Silver City way, the daughter of a rancher who runs a little starve-out spread. He said she wasn't good enough for a Krask, that I could do better. Guess he would have got over that, though, if I'd taken over the ranch. But I couldn't make myself do it. If I had, I would have messed things up right, run the place straight into the ground in no time, and ruined it for all of us. Anyway, I'd set my mind to standing on my own feet . . . and that's just what I did. Hannah and I got married. I worked around a couple of places but didn't do much good at it. About the only jobs in this country are on a ranch and that's what I didn't want. Then this town marshal job opened up. I heard about it, and, when I asked for it, they gave it to me."

"What about Big Bill . . . your pa?"

"Day I pulled out and got married, he sort of went loco. That's a little over a year ago now. He quit trying to make the ranch the biggest thing in the territory and started in . . . well, started in doing his best to become the champion hell-raiser of all time."

"Big Bill?"

"I know that's hard for you to believe, Dan, but it's the gospel truth. He's a changed man. You never saw anything like him. You think I was wild . . . you ought to take a look at him and his doings. Whiskey, women, stunts that would blunt the horns on a longhorn steer."

Big Bill Krask had apparently done a complete reversal; when he saw his fondest hopes and dreams crumble into the dust before his eyes, something within him had rebelled and broken free.

"Hard to believe," Wade murmured, thinking of the staid, dignified man he had known.

"You'll find the ranch some different, too. He's got rid of most all the old hands that had been with him for years. About the only one left is Amos Kincaid. He was riding fence for Pa when I was born . . . and my mother died. The rest quit or else were fired by him. Or were run off by his foreman. He's got a bunch of hardcases out there now, tough boys that never do a nickel's worth of work but spend their time either here in town getting drunk or else at the ranch sobering up so's they can have another go at bucking the tiger."

"Expect I met three of them tonight when I rode in," Wade said.

"That so? Catch their names?"

"A redhead they called Cully. The others were named Levi and Carl."

"They all work for Pa," Little Bill said. "Cully Brown . . . or Red, Carl Jackson, and Levi Ferrel. Blew in here from up north somewhere. Got a hunch they're the ones who hit me across the head and dumped me in that cell, but I'm not sure. Didn't see any of them. They give you much trouble?"

"Nothing serious," Dan said. "One of them mentioned a Ross. Who's he?"

"Ross Oliver, Pa's foreman. He's the headman of the bunch . . . in more ways than one."

"You said something about them jumping you before. Sounds like a regular habit."

Little Bill shook his head. "Pa makes it rough as he can for me. There's some of his crew around here every night. Then he comes in himself a couple of times a week. It's a standing order of his for the bunch to raise as much hell and create all the trouble they can. Things are getting out of hand and bound to take a bad turn, Dan. That's why I sent that letter to you."

"If he's doing it because of you,

why not move on? You could find
another job somewhere else?"

Little Bill's jaw was set. "And let
him think he'd run me off? No!
That's not the answer, anyway."

Wade studied the young lawman;
he was like his father in one respect,
bull-headed as a bogged-down year-
ling. "Kind of puts me in a crossways
bind," Dan said then, "knowing the
both of you like I do. What do you
figure I can do about it?"

Little Bill sat forward on his chair.
"Talk to Pa," he said earnestly. "He
always liked you, respected you. And
he knows you've been around. See if
you can't make him show some sense.
I've sort of side-stepped the problem
ever since it started because he is my
pa and I knew he was pulling it to
spite me. But it can't go on much

longer. I can't keep the townspeople pacified . . . they want him and his bunch kept out. So, sooner or later, there'll have to come a showdown and I don't want that, Dan . . . not with my own pa."

Wade said: "I see what you mean. But I doubt if he'll pay any mind to me."

"He just might. If there's one man alive he would listen to . . . it's you. Maybe this sounds selfish to you, but it's not only for my sake I'm asking. It's for him, too. At the rate he's going, he'll be dead in another year. A man his age, and not being used to it, can't pull what he's doing and stay alive. If the whiskey and women and hell-raising don't kill him, one of those hardcases will."

Dan looked up quickly. "Is he having trouble with some of them?"

"Not particularly, that I know of. But when they're all liquored up, some of them get plenty mean. Anything could happen."

Wade sat in silence for a long minute. Finally he nodded. "All right. I'll ride out to the ranch in the morning and see him. I'm not much of a talker when it comes to something like this, and I don't make any promise that it will do any good. I figure a man has a right to do what he pleases as long as he's willing to foot the bill."

"Bound to help," the young lawman said, showing his relief. "I'm betting he'll listen to you."

"Knowing Big Bill, I doubt if he's changed much that way, but. . . ."

The dry scuff of boot heels on the wooden landing in front of the jail halted Dan Wade's words. He saw Krask glance to the door, heard the heavy sigh that passed through his lips.

"Who is it?" Dan asked.

Little Bill shrugged. "Should have expected it," he said. "It's the citizens' delegation again."

IV

They filed quietly into the breathlessly hot room. Five men, all with drawn, serious faces. Wade immediately recognized two of their number: Kingsford who ran the hardware supply company and Tom Hotchkiss, the general merchandise store owner. They came to a halt before Little Bill's desk. Wade felt their eyes rake him, curious and wondering. He nodded briefly to them.

Krask said: "Pull up a bench, gentlemen. Make yourself comfortable."

"Won't be here long enough for that, Marshal," Hotchkiss snapped. "What we've got to say will be short and to the point."

"Figured that," Little Bill said dryly. "However, first I'd like you to meet a friend of mine. Maybe some of you already know him . . . Dan Wade."

Dan rose to his feet, extended his hand to the man nearest, Hotchkiss.

"Haven't I met you before?" the merchant asked, looking more closely into Wade's face.

"Used to work for Big Bill, on the Double K. It was several years ago."

Hotchkiss bobbed his head several times. "Sure, I recollect you now. You did a lot of riding for him."

"You probably know Mister Kingsford, too," Little Bill continued. Both Wade and the hardware store man nodded.

"Next gentlemen there is Herman Wall. Runs a hay and grain and stable place next to the Rainbow."

Wall was a squat, heavy-set person who wore blue, bib overalls and a white shirt, complete, oddly enough, with necktie. He said — "How do." — in a flat Midwestern voice.

"George Calloway," Krask said, shifting his attention to the fourth man, a tall, well-dressed, elderly individual with small, shoe-button eyes and a full, white mustache. "He's the owner of the hotel . . . the Great Western. He's the mayor, too."

"My pleasure," Wade said, taking

the man's hand. "You must have bought out Harry Miller. He ran the hotel when I was here before."

"Several years ago . . . ," Calloway murmured, and stopped.

"Aaron Leslie," the lawman concluded, coming to the last townsman. "Our lawyer and real estate agent."

Leslie was small, slight, with iron-gray hair and pale blue eyes that were sharp and probing. He shook Dan's hand with firm pressure and said nothing.

"You just riding through?" Hotchkiss asked, when the introductions were over.

Wade caught the hidden meaning in the question. The merchant just as well could have said: You interested in the marshal's job?

He smiled, returned to his chair.

"No plans. Not looking for work, either. Still a few places I haven't seen yet."

Hotchkiss said: "I see." He swiveled his eyes to Calloway. "Go ahead, George. Let's get this over and done with."

The mayor of Burnt Springs cleared his throat. "Fact is, Marshal, we came to talk about that wild bunch of your father's. They about wrecked the town again."

"Where were you when it was going on?" Herman Wall demanded. "Kept waiting for you to show up. Maybe you could have stopped them."

Little Bill looked down at his hands. "Got tied up," he said in a low voice. "Anybody hurt?"

"Roughed that hostler that works

for Garvey considerable," Hotchkiss said. "Nothing he won't live through. But something's got to be done about that crowd."

"We hired you to keep the peace around here," Calloway said. "We figured you'd be able to do it. Now, I hate to say this, Marshal, but we're wondering if we made a mistake. Maybe you're not man enough to handle the job."

"We know you got sort of a special problem," the stableman, Wall, added, "your pa being mixed up in it like he is. But that don't change things none. Either this town is law-abiding or it ain't."

"Burnt Springs is getting a bad reputation," Calloway said, picking up the conversation. "First thing you know we'll have a bunch of outlaws and drifters hanging around here, all figuring the town is a good place to hang out. We sure can't have that, Marshal. Not only would it hurt business, but it will ruin our chances for getting that other stage-line stop."

"And it will put an end to the government handling that Fort Glade payroll transfer through here, too," Wall said. "They won't be taking no chances on fifty or sixty thousand dollars gold being picked off by a gang of outlaws roosting around the town."

"Is there some talk of that?" Aaron Leslie, speaking for the first time, asked quickly.

"Not yet," Calloway admitted, "but it's bound to crop up. And if they quit sending the shipments through here, we'll stand to lose a lot of business. All those soldiers trading with our local businessmen mean plenty of extra cash changing hands. What's worse, once the word got out that the Army didn't figure Burnt Springs was a safe and law-abiding community, we'd be dead. People would avoid us like the plague. It would not only spoil our chances for the new stage stop but cause us to lose the old one as well."

A silence fell after that. The five townsmen stood before Little Bill, seemingly waiting for some statement from him. The young lawman stirred.

"I've been doing the best I could," he said, "and without any help from the town or anybody else. Little hard to get much done when you don't have some backing. And, as you said, I've had a special problem to deal with."

"Man has to put his personal troubles to one side," Wall said. "Either that or move on. Time comes when he's got to rope or brand . . . because he sure can't do the both. There's no standing still, smack in the middle."

Krask nodded. "I'm not making excuses. I think you'll agree that I've done my job most of the time, except maybe where Pa was concerned."

Calloway shook his head impatiently. "Maybe it looks that way to you, but I've got to be honest . . . we don't agree. You've got to look at this thing from the top, take an overall view. And it boils down to this. Things are getting out of hand around here. The town's going to get hurt, and, either you put a stop to it, regardless of who you tromp on, or we hire on somebody who will. We're asking you flat out if you're willing to do it or do you want us to find another man?"

Again there was silence in the stifling room. Down the street, in the Rainbow, the piano tinkled on through the muted sounds of confusion. The roan, still at the hitch rail, blew and stamped wearily. Dan waited to hear Little Bill's reply.

"I can take care of it," the young lawman said.

Wall said: "Fine. You say you can take care of it. Now we want to know how . . . and when. So far we ain't seen much sign of you enforcing the law. Like tonight. You should have been out there, dragging those hardcases off that poor boy of Garvey's."

"I would have been there," Little

Bill began, suddenly very angry, "only. . . ."

"Only what?" Calloway pressed gently.

Dan Wade could understand Little Bill's reluctance to continue the explanation — to tell how he had been attacked in the darkness, overcome, and thrown into a cell in his own jail. It would be a humiliating admission.

"Like I said, I got held up. When I did get the chance, it was too late. The Double K bunch was riding out."

Calloway shrugged. "Don't know what it was that delayed you and you don't seem anxious to talk about it, but it seems to me, Marshal, your job ought to come first, before everything else. Anyway, that's the way it has to

be from here on out. We'll be expect-
ing it."

"It's what you'll get."

"Good. Glad we understand each
other now. You said you could take
care of things but you never did
answer Herman's question . . . how
and when?"

"Beginning right now," Little Bill
said. "That covers the second part."
He half turned, ducked his head at
Wade. "He's the how of it."

Calloway swung his attention to
Dan. Interest at once broke across
the faces of Hotchkiss and Joe Kingsford.

"You hiring him on as a deputy?"
the hardware store man asked
quickly.

Wade felt the eyes of the men drilling into him. He didn't appreciate

the position into which he had been suddenly thrust, that of an outside gun being brought in to clean up a wild town. Quick denial sprang to his lips but Little Bill spoke first.

"Not exactly a deputy," he explained, "but as a friend. My pa always thought a heap of Dan. I've asked him to go talk things over with Pa, see if he couldn't settle him down a bit and make his riders behave. I think he can do it."

Disappointment was evident on the faces of the merchants. Calloway, however, did not give up. "We can use a deputy here, Wade. Any chance of you being interested?"

Dan said — "No." — immediately and firmly. "I'll leave the badge-wearing to the men who've got a liking for it. But I'll help," he added, glancing at Little Bill. "I figure to ride out and pay a call in the morning."

Calloway lifted his hands, allowed them to fall to his sides. "Well, something sure has got to be done. We can't let things go on the way they have. And, Marshal, only fair I warn you that unless you can straighten all this out, we'll be asking you for your resignation. Nothing personal, you understand, we simply have to have a man who can run things."

"I know what you mean," Little Bill said. "Don't worry about it. Things will start changing around here tomorrow."

"Hope so," the mayor said. He swung to Dan. "Glad to have met you, Wade. And good luck tomorrow when you see Krask."

Dan nodded. He shook hands all

around again, watched the townsmen walk across the room and file through the doorway. Behind him he heard the young lawman sigh thankfully and murmur: "That's over with. Dan, if you fail me tomorrow, I'm finished."

V

Dan Wade wheeled slowly. It was the Little Bill Krask of the past speaking, the humored, spoiled son of an indulgent father leaning on someone else, depending upon another to bail him out of his trouble.

"Don't bank much on me," Dan said sharply. "This is your problem and you'd better face up to it. I'll do what I can to help, but I doubt if I'll have much luck."

"Pa will listen to you," the young lawman said confidently. "He's just got to."

"What if he doesn't?"

Little Bill got to his feet, spread his hands in a gesture of hopeless resignation. "Then . . . then I guess I don't know what happens. One sure thing, I can't have a showdown with him."

"Can't or won't?" Dan asked softly,

Krask turned to him, his face pulled into a dark frown. "What's that mean?"

"Big difference in the words. Either you can't or you won't . . . which is it?"

The lawman's shoulders went down. "Maybe a little of both, Dan. Point is, it would come to gun play. The way Pa is acting, I wouldn't put it past him to draw on me. And I won't let it go that far. I can't. One thing I did learn good while I was out rousting around was how to handle a gun. Pa is good but he'd have no chance against me if I was forced to pull on him."

Dan Wade nodded thoughtfully. "I see what you're driving at," he said. He was getting a better idea of Little Bill's problem now, but it was difficult to believe there would ever come gun play between the two Krasks — between father and son.

"Past supper time," the lawman said as if suddenly aware of that fact. "Hannah will be waiting for me. How about coming along? You just rode in, so I know you haven't eaten yet."

Wade hesitated. "I'm afraid that would put your wife to a lot of bother."

"Not in the least. Besides, I want you to meet her, Dan. And you might just as well spend the night with us."

"No, I'll get a room at the Great Western," Wade said. "It'd be better for me. But I'll take you up on that supper invitation. It's been a long time since I had a good, home-cooked meal."

"Fine. Let's go then. We can walk. It's only a short way."

"Walk?" Dan echoed, having a saddleman's usual aversion to it. But he gave it a second thought, decided it wouldn't be a bad idea, if not far. The roan was tired, needed feeding. He should be in a stable.

"It'll help work up your appetite," Little Bill said cheerfully, the visit from the townsmen, the problem with his father, apparently gone from his mind. "Mite of exercise never hurt nobody."

"Couple of things I sure don't need," Wade grumbled as they passed through the doorway, "exercise and something to whet my appetite. We'll have to take this horse of mine to the stable first. He needs care worse than me."

With Little Bill at his side he led the gelding to the livery barn behind the hotel and turned him over to the hostler. After arranging for his keep, he followed Krask back into the street. They strode along through the darkness, crossed a vacant lot, and arrived at a small, white house.

It was neat and well-tended. Wild yellow roses grew thick in the front yard along with lilacs, now past their blooming but still standing, full and green. A garden, lush with growing vegetables, was visible along the south side of the building and partly across the rear. Fragrant honeysuckle trailed up the well house and other vines climbed over other small out-buildings.

"Hannah did all this," Little Bill said proudly. "It was no more than a run-down shack when we moved in. She's a real wonder when it comes to making a home."

"A man couldn't ask for a finer-looking place," Wade said.

They turned up a stone walk bordered with rows of the small purple flowers that grew on the prairies, and mounted the porch. At the sound of their boot heels on the dry boards, the door swung in.

Hannah Krask was tall, gracefully formed. She had dark hair and eyes and her skin, under the shaded lamplight, had a soft, creamy look. She was wearing a white, nicely fitting dress over which she had drawn a lace-edged apron. She smiled, moved into the circle of Little Bill's arms, and kissed him unabashedly. After a moment she turned her head, looked squarely at Dan, her eyes calm and questioning.

"The name's Wade, ma'am . . . Dan Wade," he said, removing his hat.

Krask pulled away quickly from his wife. "Oh, Hannah . . . I'm sorry. This is the friend I've told you about, the one I wrote to."

She extended her hand to Dan. "I'm happy to meet you," she said in a low, quiet voice. "Bill has told me so much about you I feel we're already friends."

"I hope we are," Dan said. "I'd sure not want it any other way."

She smiled at him, stepped back into the room. "Supper is ready. Just give me time to set another plate."

"Don't go to any trouble . . . ," Dan began.

"No trouble at all," she broke in. "If you'd care to wash up, Bill will show you where, on the back porch."

The lawman led Dan to the rear of the house where he removed the dust and sweat of the trail and made himself more presentable. As he brushed down his hair with the stiff bristle that was handy, Little Bill leaned nearer to him.

"I'd be obliged to you if you don't say anything to Hannah about me getting rapped over the head. Or about the mayor and the others paying me a call. She does enough worrying over me."

Dan said: "Sure, however you want it."

He waited while the lawman attended to his own needs. Finished, they returned to the kitchen. The meal was ready and they sat down to the table.

It was a supper Dan Wade would not soon forget. Steak, fried tender and juicy, hot biscuits and honey, sweet corn on the cob flavored with fresh butter, wilted lettuce salad, strong coffee, and steaming apple pie buttressed with crushed nuts. Hannah Krask was as adept and proficient within her home as she was outside. She blushed at the compliment.

"Now if you men will go into the parlor, I'll clean up my dishes," she said when the final cup of coffee had been drunk.

"Can't you let them go . . . at least for a while?" Little Bill asked.

"Only take me a minute," she replied. "I never like to think of dirty dishes, waiting in a pan."

Dan trailed Krask into the front part of the house, sank into one of the rocking chairs. "Haven't eaten like that in years," he said. "Your wife has a way with vittles."

"She has a way with everything," Little Bill said. "I'm a right lucky man."

"For a fact."

"Big reason why I've got to straighten things up around here. I want to keep my job so we can stay here in Burnt Springs."

"Then make up your mind to it," Dan said. "Don't let anybody force you to do something you're set against."

"Meaning Pa?"

"Him or anybody else. Most men spend a lifetime hunting for what they want. Appears to me you've already found it. Now all you've got to do is fight to hold it."

"But against my own pa. . . ."

"It's a choice you'll have to make. It will either be Hannah and your life, or knuckling under to Big Bill and doing what he says, his way. It's a hard thing to decide, but you'll have to do it."

"I never looked at it quite that way, but I reckon you're right."

"I know I'm right," Dan said. He pulled himself up from the comfort of the chair. "Guess this won't show off my manners as any great shakes, but I'd best be getting back to the hotel. I'd hate to fall asleep here where I'm sitting. I've been in the saddle since before sunrise and I'm beginning to feel the miles."

"It's all right. I understand."

Dan rose to his feet. "I'll say my thanks to your wife again, and a good night." He walked to the kitchen, paused in the doorway. "I'll be going, Missus Krask."

She turned, gave him her smile. "Please call me Hannah, Dan. And you're welcome. I heard what you said. It always pleases me to see a man enjoy his food." She wiped her hands on the apron, moved nearer to him. "I want to thank you for the things you said to Bill. About his father, I mean. It's his biggest problem . . . and perhaps his greatest fault."

"He'll work it out," Dan murmured. "I'll help."

"I hope you can," she said. "I love him very much and he's a fine man. If only. . . ."

"If only what?"

"If he could just learn to stand on his own feet, depend on himself. He has the ability, but somehow he can't seem to find himself."

"I know what you mean," Wade said. "But worrying about it won't help any."

"I know that, and I sha'n't . . . now that you're here. But, in a way, I'm sorry you came."

"Sorry?"

"Yes. Now he can depend on you. Maybe, if you hadn't received that letter of his, he would have found a way to meet his troubles himself."

"I wouldn't worry about that much, either," Dan said. "If I know Big Bill, he won't listen much to what I've got to say. I doubt if it'll make the slightest difference to him."

Hannah's eyes clouded. "Don't you really think so? Bill is planning so strongly on it."

Wade stared at her, momentarily speechless. The paradoxical stream of her thoughts, of woman's logic almost halted him in his tracks. In one breath the practical Hannah was hoping the man she loved would stand on his own feet, face his own problems; in the next she was expressing her fears that outside aid would not be of benefit to him. He shook his head.

"I expect there's no point in stewing about it now. I'm going to see Big Bill tomorrow and we'll know then for certain. Thank you again, Hannah, for the fine meal and your hospitality."

"You're more than welcome, Dan. Please come often."

He made his farewell to Little Bill, promising to meet him as soon as he returned from his visit to the Double K, and started back through the warm darkness for the hotel. He was considering his own problems now, what had to be done if Big Bill refused to mend his ways, or even talk about it, which would likely prove the case. What course could he then follow?

He was standing squarely in the middle of the controversy — a position he disliked intensely — and he was almost to the point of echoing Hannah Krask's wish that he had never received Little Bill's letter. But he had, and now his sense of obligation would not permit him to brush it aside, wash his hands of the trouble, and ride on.

He reached the rear of Kingsford's place, walked up the narrow weed- and trash-filled passageway that lay between it and the adjoining structure, the ladies' dress shop. Little Bill and Hannah had their personal rights, their license to live as they wished, and it should be respected by everyone, including Big Bill. But he could sympathize with the elder Krask, even partially understand his determination to punish, in some way, his son. That was wrong, of course, and Big Bill should be made to see it.

He gained the street, deserted now, and swung toward the Great Western. The Rainbow was still going strong, all windows ablaze with light, music blaring from the doorway, loud talking and laughing seeping through the walls. He considered, briefly, the need for a drink — it might drive the stiffness from his bones, loosen his muscles — and then dismissed it. A bed was what he really desired. After the long day and the fine meal Hannah had placed before him, he. . . .

He heard the sharp, wicked crack of a pistol, the dull thud of a bullet smash into the wall only inches from his head. For an instant he remained motionless, startled, completely taken off guard. Then it drove into his mind; someone was shooting at him. He hit the ground in a quick, flat drive.

VI

He rolled into the black shadows along the front of the dress shop, straining his eyes to locate the ambusher. The shot had apparently gone unnoticed, for the piano in the Rainbow hammered on relentlessly and no one came through the batwings to investigate. It was understandable. The sound of a single pistol report was no uncommon thing; only a flurry of shots would be likely to draw attention.

He had not the vaguest notion where the bullet had been fired from — or who could have sent it searching for his life. He had no enemies in Burnt Springs, at least none of whom he was aware. And during the short time he had been in the settlement that day he had met only five merchants. That one of them should want to kill him was scarcely logical. The trio of cowpunchers who had jumped him. He had forgotten them — the redhead, Cully Brown, and his friends, Carl and Levi. It had to be one of them. Most likely it was Cully. He again searched the street for some sign of the man, concentrating particularly on that area to the right of the Rainbow. There was a passageway between that hulking building and its neighbor, Garvey's Livery Stable.

Such a place would be ideal for a man to hide and maintain a close view of the street.

He could do no good lying there in the dark. And if he got to his feet, the hidden marksman, if he were still nearby, could pick him off with ease. But the angry impatience of the man would not permit him to remain there in the dust indefinitely. Gun in hand, and still prone, he began to work his way backward. Keeping close to the wall of the dress shop, he watched the street as he labored through the loose, yellowish powder that sucked into his throat and nostrils, threatening to choke him. Finally he was abreast the passageway. Still flat on his belly, he twisted about and crawled into its black depths.

He rose to his feet quickly, ran

swiftly to the rear of the buildings, his shoulders slamming alternately against Kingsford's and the dress shop's walls as he plunged heedlessly on. He turned right at the end of the dark corridor, hurried along the alleyway that cut across the backs of the structures, until he came to where it ended, in intersection with the cross street. He was at the northwest corner of Hotchkiss's store at this point, with the Rainbow, Garvey's, and the other small places just opposite.

There he halted. He should continue on, he knew, circle the Rainbow and come up behind the stable. But the instant he moved out of the shadows back of the Hotchkiss building, he would be fully exposed. He stood there in the night, smoldering and disturbed, debating the question. And then abruptly it was solved for him. Beyond Garvey's he heard the quick rush of a horse getting away fast. Dan stood perfectly quiet for several moments and listened to the rapid hammering of hoof beats striking north. He realized then the ambusher had given it up.

He walked into the open, convinced but still on the alert. There was no blast of gunfire from the passageway next to the Rainbow, or from any other position of advantage; there was only the racket from the saloon and in that he found no interest. He continued on to the Great Western, going first to the stable for his saddlebags and to check on the roan. The big gelding was enjoying his rest and Dan crossed the yard and entered the hotel by its rear door. A middle-aged clerk with black, patent-leather hair parted exactly in the center greeted him sourly at the desk and assigned him to Room 5.

He undressed and went immediately to bed, his thoughts swirling about the two Krasks, about Hannah, and about the man in the night who had fired a bullet at him. He was still convinced it was one of the three cowpunchers he had encountered earlier in the evening, with the redheaded Cully Brown being the most logical suspect. In any event, Cully was due to supply some answers.

He awakened early, shaved, bathed as best he could from the tin wash pan and china pitcher of water, and pulled on clean clothing. He went down into the street and turned left for the Chicago Café. The owner-cook-waiter served him bacon, eggs, and coffee in the grumpy silence of a man who had risen too early, too often, and then left him entirely alone. Dan ate slowly, far from hungry after the huge meal he had enjoyed that previous night at the Krasks'.

That over, he returned to the Great Western and cut around to its rear to the stable. He sought out the roan and looked him over carefully. The hostler had done a good job on the horse, currying and brushing him down until his coat was sleek and smooth. The grain and fresh hay Wade had ordered and the night's rest had put him in top condition.

Dan was throwing on his gear when the stableman appeared. He watched for a few moments, then finally spoke.

"Be right glad to do that for you, mister, but I'd guess you're a man who likes to do his own saddling up."

"You'd be right," Wade said. "The roan's got touchy withers. The saddle has to set just so."

"Be no change in the price, your doin' your own hostlin'."

"Suits me," Dan said, and went on with his chore. A thought struck him. "You happen to be around here last night, say about nine o'clock?"

"Reckon I was. Why?"

"Hear some shooting? One shot. Sounded like it came from across the way, maybe that passage between Garvey's and the Rainbow."

"Sure, I heard it."

Wade paused. "See who it was?"

The stableman shrugged. "Didn't bother to look. Shootin' like that goes on around here all the time. Drunks, mostly, blowin' off steam. Wonder more people don't get hurt. It bother you?"

Dan resumed his task. He had the saddle on to his and the roan's satisfaction, turned now to the silver-mounted bridle. "No reason. Just wondered what it was all about."

"One of that crowd from the Double K, I'd reckon. Rode north when he left. You pullin' out today."

"No, I'll be around for a spell. You want your money now or when I settle up with the hotel?"

The hostler studied Wade for a time. Then: "Guess you might as well wait. You don't look like a man who'd beat a stable bill."

"Thanks," Dan said dryly and swung up onto the roan. He wheeled the big horse about, trotted him down the runway, and out into the street. He turned right, rounded the corner, and pointed north. It was a two-hour ride to the Double K but with the gelding feeling as he did, they likely would make it in less.

Familiar sights began to greet him as he rode steadily along through the sweet, early morning freshness. The stand of red buttes off to the right, the long, twisting band of green cottonwood trees that grew on the ragged banks of Copper Mine Creek. He crossed the deep wash where once he had killed a cougar just after it had struck down a calf, climbed the rocky slope where he had been thrown by a balky mustang and sustained a broken arm. At the top was the gnarled, brushy cedar where he had seen Big Bill shoot down a rustler.

Other places came before him, passed on as he followed the well-traveled road, and he fell to wondering just how things might have been with him had he stayed with Krask and not ridden on that spring morning when the urge to drift had gotten so strong he could no longer deny it. Probably he would have been the foreman of the Double K by now — or he could have gained nothing. When the break between father and son had come, he would have been hard put to hold his tongue with Big Bill.

The miles wore on as the heat increased. He reached the last long grade to the ridge and began the gentle but steady climb. The roan scarcely slowed when he started up but continued on in that easy, rocking lope that covered distance so efficiently. From the top Dan would look down upon the broad, green valley in which the ranch lay, a fine, beautiful sight that fairly took a man's breath away. He had sat there often in the old days, just drinking in the view. There had been times when he had thought of finding such a valley and claiming it for his own. He would build himself a ranch, find a woman he could love and who loved him, and settle down. But it had never come to pass; he had never discovered the valley or the woman, either, and thus had wandered on through the years, happy, he supposed, with his way of life, often lonely, especially after seeing the luck others, like Little Bill, had been fortunate enough to encounter. But he was never completely satisfied with himself. Deep in his mind he knew the answer, the cure for it all, yet he could never bring himself to accepting and following it to its conclusion. What he did not know was the reason why, and in that lay his fears.

He gained the summit, halted. Magnificent Cloud River Valley unfurled below him, rolling endlessly out to all sides in a pale green sea of sweet, tender grass, but there was something wrong, something strange in the picture. He considered it in silence for a time, and then realized what was missing — there were no cattle, no grazing herds scattered here and there over the land.

Pondering that singularity, he put the roan into motion and started down into the valley. A few minutes later he heard hoof beats and again drew to a stop, listening. Several riders were coming toward him. He wheeled the gelding off the road and into a stand of brush to wait, not afraid, simply curious.

It was Cully Brown and the same two who had been with him the night before, Levi Ferrel and Carl Jackson. They were obviously heading for Burnt Springs, and Little Bill's remark relative to the amount of work his father's cowpunchers did on the Double K flipped back into Dan Wade's mind. But he had other thoughts about these three. He waited until they were just past him and then rode out into the center of the lane.

"Hold it!" he barked, drawing his gun. "Raise your hands high and turn around . . . slow."

They obeyed instantly, finding the cold tone of his voice entirely convincing. When they saw Wade, their surprise was evident. Apparently whoever had fired the shot in the dark had assumed he had hit his target and had so informed his friends. Wade, his face set in hard, humorless lines, pushed up nearer.

"One of you bushwhackers took a shot at me last night," he said. "The bullet missed. I figure I ought to give whichever one of you it was another try."

There was no answer.

Wade said: "Ought to be easier. Man can see better . . . and it's three to one. How about you, redhead?"

"Who said it was me?" Cully demanded, instantly aroused.

"Nobody . . . yet," Dan replied coolly. "Was it?"

"You don't know who it was," Levi said, relaxing in his saddle. "You're just guessin', runnin' a bluff, tryin' to find out which. . . ."

"Shut up!" Cully broke in, grinding out the words. "Keep your lip buttoned."

"He's right, redhead," Dan said. "I'm just fishing, but I know it was one of you. When I find out which, that man's getting his second chance whether he wants it or not. Nobody takes a shot at me without I get my turn, too. Now, head back for the ranch. I want Big Bill to know all about this before it happens."

Cully Brown stared at Wade blankly for a long moment, then he grinned faintly. "Sure. Whatever you want," he said, and moved off down the road. The others followed immediately.

They descended the long slope, the three abreast with Dan, gun in hand, behind a few paces. They crossed the quarter mile of open flats and turned into the yard, riding through the familiar high gate with its two interlocked Ks still hanging by chains from the crosspiece.

"Pull up in front of the house," Wade said, motioning with his weapon.

The three riders obediently angled across the hard pack, halted at the hitch rail that stood before the long, low, rambling structure.

"Just sit easy," Dan said, "while I. . . ."

"While you do what, friend?" a harsh voice demanded from the far end of the building.

Wade swung his glance to that point, watched a small, thin-faced man with leveled rifle bearing straight at his breast ease into view. There were soft sounds at the opposite corner. Two more men, guns glinting in the sunlight, showed themselves. Beyond them, coming from the bunkhouse, were three others. The Double K was an armed camp.

"One thing you'd sure better do," the man with the rifle said, "is drop that pistol. You make one wrong move with it and we'll blow you clean off that saddle!"

VII

Dan Wade let the .44 fall to the ground. He heard Cully laugh, saw the redhead twist about. "Was hopin' you'd see us comin', Ross," he said. "This here's that drifter we told you about."

Ross — Ross Oliver. This was Big Bill's foreman. He looked more like a gunman gambler, of the kind who frequented the saloons along the cattle trails.

"Sure goin' to have me some fun now," Cully said, his face evil and expectant. "You all just stand around and do the watchin'. I got a score to settle."

The men with the drawn weapons closed in from either side. Dan remained still, waited out the tight moments. Cully swung down from his horse, made a great show of looping his reins about the rail. Carl and Levi followed. Ross Oliver came to a quiet stop a dozen paces away.

"You didn't do so good last night," the foreman said, looking at the redhead. "And you had plenty of help."

"Grabbed me when I wasn't watchin'. Be another story out here."

"Maybe. Who is he?"

"Nobody much. Just some drifter. Was hangin' around the kid."

Oliver shifted his expressionless face to Dan. "You got a name?" he demanded in a harsh, brittle way.

Wade nodded. "Most men do. Call Big Bill out here and let him tell it to you."

"You know the old man?"

"He'll answer that, too."

Oliver hesitated momentarily. He nodded to Carl. "Go get him. He's inside."

Jackson swung obediently for the house. He entered, slammed the screen door behind him.

From where he stood near the hitch rack, Cully said: "You just remember, Ross, this jasper belongs to me. Few things I'm goin' to learn him."

The foreman said — "Sure, sure." — in a patient way. "You'll have to do better than you did last night, howsoever."

"Told you he jumped me when I wasn't lookin'."

"Not the way I heard it."

The screen banged again. Dan threw his glance toward the house. Two men were on the gallery that ran the full width of the house — Carl and a large, heavily built man dressed in ill-fitting, wrinkled clothing. His hair was long, badly needing the attentions of a barber. A week's growth of beard covered his slack face and he swayed slightly as he stared vacantly at Dan.

"What's this all about? What's the trouble here, Ross?"

Even the voice was different, no longer brisk and authoritative. It now bordered on the querulous, almost plaintive. But there was no mistaking Big Bill Krask.

"Drifter crossing our land," Ross Oliver said. "Claims to be a friend of yours."

"Friend?" the cattleman echoed. "Friend of mine?"

He came off the porch, crossed the

interval of yard at an unsteady shamble. Dan watched him in silence, appalled at the vast change that had taken place in the man. Krask halted at the hitch rack, focusing his eyes after some difficulty upon Wade. He jerked himself upright suddenly.

"Dan Wade! You're damn' right he's my friend!" he shouted. "Put those guns away! What the hell's wrong with all you, anyway?"

Oliver lowered his rifle slowly, reluctantly. The other men watched him closely. At his nod they, too, holstered their weapons.

"Just being careful," the foreman said.

"Hell of a note when a man's friends can't even ride by without getting throwed down on," Big Bill grumbled. "Step down, Dan! Come inside and have a drink with me!"

Wade came off the roan, scooped up his gun, and slid it back into the leather. He reached forward, took Krask's outstretched hand.

"What you doing back in this country, boy? You looking for a job? Best damn' cowhand I ever had around here," he added, throwing a side glance to Ross Oliver. "He wants work, he's hired. You understand?"

"Sure, boss, if you say so."

Krask halted abruptly, looked around the yard. "What's all these men doing here? Why ain't they out on the range where they belong? Damn it, Ross, its your job to see they keep working!"

"They're working," the foreman said, his narrow face angry. "Just happened they all dropped by at the same time. I'll get them back in the saddle, don't you worry."

"I ain't worrying," Krask said. "That's your job, Mister Oliver, running this place for me. And doing all the worrying about it. Now see they hop to it or, by God, there'll be some new hands around here! Come on, boy," he finished, grasping Wade by the arm. "No sense standing out here in this heat."

The change in Big Bill was unbelievable, and pitiful. Dan felt his heart throb as he watched the once proud man he had known stagger through the doorway, collide with one side of the frame, reel, recover, and lurch on. He led Dan through the front room, a dusty, littered parlor, into a second that served as an office. Krask collapsed into one of the several leather chairs, pointed to another.

"Set down, boy," he said, reaching for a bottle on a nearby table, "and have yourself a drink. No glasses, unless you want to trot back to the kitchen and get one."

"This suits me," Dan said, accepting the bottle. He turned it to his lips, took a swallow of the raw, fiery liquid, and handed it back to the cattleman.

Big Bill downed a hugh gulp, paused, stared at Dan. "Where you been keeping yourself, boy? Where you headed?"

"Just rode into town yesterday," Wade replied, skirting the question. "Put up at the Great Western."

"Now, why'd you do that? Why

didn't you come on out here? Always got a bed waiting for an old friend."

"Hotel's all right."

Krask had fallen silent, his swollen, glazed eyes on the floor. After a moment he said: "You see Little Bill?"

Dan nodded. "Had supper with him and his wife last night. She's a fine woman."

The rancher said nothing. He took another sip of the whiskey. "Maybe, I wouldn't be knowing about that. But he sure ain't no fine son."

"You've got him all wrong," Dan said quietly. "It wasn't right to try and make him live the kind of a life you wanted. A man can't do that, and you know it."

"He should have stayed with me. This place was his, lock, stock, and tar bucket. Always was. What the hell you think I was working and slaving all those years for? Just so's he could step into my boots."

"It doesn't always turn out the way a man hopes. People are different, even fathers and sons. He didn't take a fancy to cattle raising the way you did."

"The place was for him," Krask muttered. "Damn it, he ought to appreciate it. I worked like a dog after his ma died, fixing things so's he'd always have something good. Then he turns his back on me and walks off to some piddling job."

"It's his life . . . and what he wanted."

"It was a fool thing for him to do and I'm thinking he's sorry he ever did it."

"Don't count on it," Dan said.

"You're acting like it's the first time it ever happened. It's sure not, and it's no reason for you to carry on like you're doing. The way things are going, you'll be dead in a year, broke even sooner."

Krask sat up. He clamped his slack lips shut, glared at Dan. "You lecturing me, boy? You trying to tell grandma how to pick ducks?"

"I'm trying to make you see what's happening to you."

"Forget it. I know what I'm doing. Had my nose to the stone for thirty years building this place. Worked like a mule. Never had no time for anything. Then it turns out it was all for nothing. Now, I'm having myself a right good time. I'm sowing plenty of those wild oats you hear tell about. Why not? Sure ain't no reason for me to keep on grubbing away. I'm catching up on all the fun I missed while Little Bill was growing up."

"And digging your grave fast as you can."

"Maybe so. But who cares?"

"Little Bill, for one, and probably a few others, not including that foreman you've got running the spread or those hardcases he's hired on."

"You mean Ross? What's wrong with him? He's looking after things, doing what Little Bill ought to be doing. And the boys . . . they're all right. Maybe a mite on the tough side but they get the job done and they're powerful good hands to go to town with. They know how to have a good time . . . something I've had to learn."

"It could be they know a lot about other things, too, like how to steal a man blind. You getting out of cattle business?"

"Me? Hell no!"

"I sure didn't see any stock when I rode in. How many head are you running?"

Krask wagged his head. "Last tally run close to three thousand, Ross said."

"Must all be on the north range," Dan said. "They're sure not around anywhere else. Had a good look at the valley from the ridge."

Krask moved his hand in a wide gesture. "They're somewhere. I ain't worrying about it. That's Ross Oliver's job."

"Maybe he's doing it. I'm hoping."

The rancher lapsed again into a moody silence. He offered the bottle to Dan who refused. He took a long swig, lowered the glass container, and stared at it.

"Little Bill talk about me any?"

"Some. He wanted me to do a little jawing with you."

"About what?"

"About the way you're acting, the way you and your crew keep hurrahing the town. He's going to lose out sure on that marshal job unless you quit it. Could even come to worse."

"Hope he does lose that tin star. Then maybe he'll come home where he belongs."

"No chance of that. If you cause him to fail, he's liable to pick up and move on. He's as bull-headed as you. One thing of yours he got."

"Then let him move. Let him get clean out of the country. I ain't hankering to set eyes on him . . . and you can tell him so. And while you're at it, tell him something else. Tomorrow is Saturday, my special day to howl. I'll be in with the boys and we aim to tree that town for fair. Been a lot of talking about me going on and there's a few who's about to eat their words. You tell that biggety marshal that for me, boy."

"Don't do it," Dan said. "Don't push things too far. It could mean real trouble."

"Trouble! That's something that boy ain't seen yet! Long as he keeps wearing that star, it's going to get worse and worse."

Dan rose to his feet. He turned abruptly, caught the swift motion of shadow in the hallway. Someone had been listening, watching. He thought for a moment, came back to Big Bill.

"I'm asking you again, friend to friend, forget about coming to town tomorrow. Let it ride this time."

"Nope, we'll be there. Them dudes have a lesson coming to them and they're sure going to get it. You leaving?"

"Time to head back," Dan said, moving toward the door. "I hate to see you in such rough shape, Big Bill. It's not much like it used to be."

"Everything's changed," Krask said. "You going to be around tomorrow? I'd like to buy you a drink."

"Expect I'll be there," Wade replied. "One thing more, if you bring that redhead, Cully Brown, in with you, better tell him to watch his step."

"So? What's he up to?"

"Somebody took a shot at me in the dark last night. I figure it was him.

112

He makes one more mistake like that he'll be looking at the business end of my forty-four."

"That danged fool," Krask muttered. "Never does show much sense. I'll jack him up a mite about it."

"Good enough," Dan said, and walked on toward the front door. The hall was empty.

VIII

Dan Wade halted when he stepped out onto the gallery. He was wary, alert for trouble. He could expect it from Ross Oliver, from Cully and the others. That he was at odds with the redhead and his pals was enough but the fact that he was an old family friend of Big Bill's and thus represented a threat to whatever was going on at the Double K heightened the probabilities. The yard was deserted. Even the horses of the three riders were gone. Only the roan stood at the hitch rack, dozing as he waited in the bright, hot sun.

Nerves fiddle-string tight, Dan stepped off the porch and crossed to the horse. He jerked the leathers free, swung onto the saddle. From somewhere within the house there was a sudden crash, a shattering of glass. Either Big Bill had dropped his bottle, likely empty, or in a fit of anger had hurled it against the wall.

He wheeled the roan about, starting for the distant slope. His back was to the ranch buildings now, prime target for anyone lurking about who had a wish to see him dead. He rode straight on, wide shoulders square against the horizon. He could feel the hair on his neck prickling, the tauntness of his singing nerves, but he did not look back.

Whoever had been hiding in the hall at Big Bill Krask's had heard all that had been said. It could have been Ross Oliver, or it might have been Cully or another of the crew. Regardless, the foreman would know now that Krask still hoped for his son's return, that despite all the loud talk and threats the cattleman still had dreamed of the day when Little Bill would take over the Double K. And he would also know that Dan Wade was a close friend, near to the problem, and one who could possibly effect a reconciliation. Thus, to Oliver's way of thinking, he would be a most unwelcome visitor to Cloud

River Valley and Burnt Springs.

He reached the gate, broke onto the broad flats. Only then did he touch the roan with his spurs, send the big gelding into a long lope. After that he began to breathe easier.

To his way of thinking the visit with Big Bill had been a complete failure. He had feared it would be. He had accomplished nothing other than to verify the things the young marshal had told him had come to pass — and to add a further conviction to his fund of information. Ross Oliver and his hardcases were milking the Double K dry. And to do so they were keeping the cattleman in such a state of mind and alcoholism that he was totally unaware of what was happening. Just exactly what Oliver was doing was difficult to say at this

point; it would bear looking into at
the first possible moment, Dan decided. First, however, must come
Little Bill's problems and his need
for help. That a clash between the
two was in the offing, possibly the
very next day, seemed inevitable.

Dan saw movement ahead on the
trail that led to the ridge. He slowed
the roan, his eyes straining ahead to
pick up, isolate the object. A rider. A
man on a small calico horse. He
studied the distant figure for some
time, endeavoring to recognize the
person. He was too far away, and,
waiting in the dappled shade of a
juniper tree, his face was indefinite.
He appeared to be making no effort
to hide, however. It could be a trick.
Dan realized that, but there was little
he could do about it. The trail was

the only way out of the valley and he had not the slightest desire to turn back. He drew his pistol, thrust it into his waistband where it would be more readily available, and rode on.

When he was within a hundred yards, he recognized the rider — Amos Kincaid. He spurred the roan forward. Kincaid, according to Little Bill, was the last of the cowpunchers who had worked for Krask from the beginning. Dan had always liked the crusty old wrangler and was glad to see him. He wheeled in to the man with his arm outstretched.

"Amos, good to see a familiar face around here."

"Reckon I'm the only one," Kincaid said, wrapping his bone-like fingers around those of Wade. "Maybe you think I ain't plumb pleasured to see you."

"Didn't notice you back at the house," Dan said. "I knew you were still working. Little Bill told me."

"I keep away from that nest of polecats much as I can. Me and them don't mix-up atall. You heading for town? Reckon I'll just mosey along with you for a spell. You been talkin' to Big Bill?"

"Some. He wasn't in much shape to hear me."

"Never is no more. Stays liquored up all the time, seems."

"What's going on back there, Amos? I mean besides the way Big Bill is carrying on. That bunch he's got working for him looks more like the Hole-in-the-Wall gang than plain 'punchers."

"Just what they are. And they're

stealin' him blind. Bet there ain't a thousand beeves left on the Double K. Ross and his crowd keeps sellin' them off, a jag at a time, and pocketin' the cash."

"Doesn't Krask realize that?"

"Don't know. I tried to tell him myself and got no place, except for lettin' myself in for a workin' over by that redhead, Cully."

"Big Bill wouldn't listen to you?"

The old cowpuncher cocked his head to one side. "You have any luck makin' him listen to you?"

"Not any," Dan replied.

"Reckon that's your answer. He lets Ross run the place, do as he pleases. He can sign the bills of sale and carry on the business the way he wants. And he don't cotton to nobody stickin' their nose into what he's doin'. Don't know what happened when you rode in back there, but I'm guessin' you was mighty lucky Big Bill was home."

"You're right. I had a few bad minutes while I thought I was going to have to fight Oliver and his whole crowd. You say Big Bill stays drunk like that all the time?"

"I can't hardly recollect seein' him sober since the day the boy pulled out. Broke the old man's heart sure enough, that did. But you ain't sayin' nothin' about yourself? What brung you back here?"

"I had a letter from Little Bill. He was hoping I could talk to his pa, straighten him out."

"He's a good boy," Kincaid said. "Big Bill sure ain't doin' the right thing by him. The kid weren't cut out to be no rancher, but Big Bill won't swaller it. Churnin' up to bad trouble between them I fear. Sure is a sad thing."

"It could get worse," Dan murmured. "Unless I miss my guess this thing is jockeying around into a gunfight."

Kincaid nodded slowly. "Ross'd like that. Them Krasks are just like a couple knot-head longhorns. Ain't neither one of them going to give an inch. The boy startin' to get riled?"

"Not so much that. It's the merchants. They served notice on him either to tame Big Bill and his bunch, or move on. He's made up his mind he's going to stay."

"Then we're sure pointin' for trouble," the old cowpuncher said, his long face solemn. "I can tell you this. Big Bill ain't goin' to pull in his horns none. He'll make it hard on the boy long as he can. He's got things all mixed up in his mind but he thinks he can make the boy come back if he rides him hard enough. You got any ideas what we ought to be doin' about it?"

"None," Dan said. "Little Bill's thinking is messed up, too. He won't move, yet he won't fight his pa. Don't know what he'll do when I tell him what Big Bill said. You be in town tomorrow?"

"Weren't figurin' on it. Reckon I can be if you say so."

"Might be a good idea. Could be I'll need some help and you're the only one I can trust."

"I'll be there, son," Kincaid said promptly. "If it comes to shootin', whose side we goin' to be on?"

Wade shook his head. "Nobody's, I hope. The thing we got to do is stop it before it starts."

They rode on in silence for another quarter mile. Kincaid reined in. "S'pect I'd better be cuttin' back right about here. Supposed to be ridin' the south range . . . what for I sure don't know. Ain't no cow critters around nowhere."

Dan reached for the old cowpuncher's hand. "So long, Amos. See you tomorrow . . . and ride careful."

"*Adiós,*" Kincaid replied. "You be doin' some of the same. The way it appears to me, you ain't so popular with Ross and his boys, either."

There was little doubt of that, Dan thought, as he put the roan to a lope. Oliver would resent any of Big Bill's old friends, knowing they would represent a threat to whatever schemes he had in mind. And it could even go deeper, he realized. Ross could be at the bottom of the continuing ill-feeling between the rancher and his son, whetting the trouble, egging Big Bill on to do something drastic. It would fit neatly into whatever plans he had.

IX

He reached Burnt Springs at noon with the hot sun drilling down with its full intensity. He went first to the hotel livery barn, stabled the gelding, then on to his room. He washed away the dust, thinking all the while on what he would tell Little Bill when he saw him. He was still undecided when he finally left the building and made his way to the lawman's office.

The marshal was not alone. A squat, heavily built man with dark hair and flat, gray eyes occupied one of the chairs. He was handsomely dressed in a broadcloth suit, fancy, handmade boots, and wore a wide-brimmed, pearl-gray hat.

Little Bill leaped to his feet as Dan entered. A smile crossed his lips and an expectant, hopeful look spread across his face.

"You see him?"

Dan nodded, halted in the center of the room.

"What happened? What did he say? You have any luck with him?"

Wade said: "None. He won't listen. Fact is, he'll be in tomorrow with his crew and they're figuring to take the town apart."

Little Bill's shoulders sagged. "Might have known it," he said in a low voice. His glance halted on the well-dressed stranger. "Oh, Dan, I'd like to have you meet Luke Grover. He's a U.S. marshal. This is Dan Wade, old friend of mine, Marshal."

Grover leaned forward, extended his hand to Wade. "Pleasure," he murmured. Then: "What's this about somebody taking the town apart? Is it something I ought to know?"

"My pa," Little Bill said, dropping back into his chair.

"Damn," Grover said under his breath. "Sure don't want that if we can help it."

Dan faced the lawman. "You here for something special, Marshal?"

"Plenty special," Grover replied.

"The Army gold shipment is due here tomorrow sometime," Little Bill explained. "Word got back to the authorities about how things here in Burnt Springs were going. They sent him to take over."

"We got a tip there might be a try at highjacking the shipment," Grover added. "Nothing definite, you understand. Only a rumor, but since there's a lot of extra cash money involved this time, they figured we'd better take no chances."

"You come alone?" Wade asked.

Grover nodded. "Didn't want to draw attention. Besides, with the marshal here and maybe one deputy, we can look after matters. Then there'll be the soldiers. I understand Major Ives usually sends a full patrol."

The federal lawman got to his feet, strolled nervously to the door, and glanced out into the street. "Hearing about your father complicates things some. With him and half a dozen of his crew tearing things wide open. . . ."

"You know about Big Bill?" Dan asked, wondering how word of the cattleman's activities could have spread so far.

Grover shrugged. "More rumors, that's all. It got to us in a roundabout way. They said he runs with a pretty wild bunch and generally put things in an uproar. It would be a good time for a gang of outlaws to hit."

The government man was right, of course. Such a moment would be ideal for a raid. But there would have to be some prearranged plan; they would need to know the gold shipment would be in town, that Big Bill and his crew were due. He turned to the young lawman.

"Did the rest of the town hear about the shipment coming in?" he asked.

"Probably. It arrives about the same time every month. The mayor knows. He talked with Grover."

The word would spread. There was no hope now of surprise or of keeping it under cover. "I expect we'd better start getting things ready then," he said.

Little Bill, still downcast, said: "How?"

"First thing we should take a look around the town, see if there's any strangers. If there are, we'll send them packing unless they've got a good reason for being here."

"Good idea," Grover said. He looked at Dan, smiled. "You'd make a good lawman, friend. How about serving as a deputy until this is over with?"

Quick refusal leaped to Dan Wade's mind, but he held back the actual words. With matters shaping up as they were, Little Bill would need all the help he could get, and perhaps he would be in better position to do something about the elder Krask, too, if he wore a star. He glanced at the young lawman. "It's all right with me, if you want it."

Little Bill smiled. "You bet I do. Starting right now."

He reached into the top drawer of the desk and procured the badge of authority. He handed it to the tall rider. "I'm swearing you in as of this moment."

Dan pinned on the star. "I never thought I'd be wearing one of these things," he said.

Grover laughed. "There's worse things," he said. "Maybe not many, but a few." He brushed back his coat. Sunlight glinted against his own badge, touched the metal of the gun at his hip. "The heat's mighty bad around here," he said. "I think I'll head on down to the hotel. It ought to be a bit cooler there. I'll leave you two to work out the details for tomorrow."

He smiled, nodded, stepped out into the street. Little Bill waited until he was gone, then spoke.

"Pa couldn't pick a worse time to come in. Why the hell couldn't that gold shipment get here today?"

"Things just happen sometimes," Wade said. "Tell me how it works. A stage brings in the money. A patrol from Fort Glade meets it and takes it over. Is that it?"

"That's about the way it goes. Sometimes we have to hold the shipment overnight. The soldiers don't always make it here at the same time the stage arrives. Once in a while they're a day early, or a day late. When that happens, we put the gold in the bank vault."

"Where does the stage stop?"

"Goes straight to the bank. There won't be any passengers. It's a special run."

"How many guards aboard?"

"One riding shotgun with the driver. Two more inside with the money."

"That ought to be plenty of help."

"You can't figure on them. Once they unload, they're through with it. Their responsibility ends there, and they seem mighty glad of it. They usually arrive late in the afternoon and turn right around and head back toward El Paso. I figure they don't want to be on hand if anything goes wrong."

"I can understand that. They're probably acting under orders. If they were around, somebody might claim they still were in charge of the shipment, if it got lost."

"Must be something to this rumor of a hold-up, them sending Grover here."

"It looks that way," Dan agreed. "The sooner we start getting set for it, the better off we'll be. The first thing we do is drop by all the saloons and check the hotels. We want to see who's in town."

Little Bill arose. "It could wait until tonight. Might be somebody'll ride in late."

"We'll make the rounds again after dark, and a couple more times tomorrow. It's best we look behind every bush . . . and keep on looking."

"I expect you're right," the lawman said, reaching for his hat. "About Pa . . . how was he?"

Wade hesitated. Then: "Same as usual, I reckon."

"Don't hold back on me!" Little Bill exclaimed, suddenly angry. "I know what he's like. Was he bad drunk?"

"Pretty bad shape," Dan said.

"Couldn't get him to make much sense. You know anything for sure about Ross Oliver, that foreman he's got? Or the rest of the bunch that works for him?"

"Only what I've told you. Ross runs the place to suit himself and Pa leaves it up to him."

"My guess is they're stealing Big Bill blind. Amos thinks so, too. Ran into him on the way back. All the time I was in the valley I never saw a steer."

"That's what I've been figuring, too. But how are you going to make Pa see it when he plain doesn't want to . . . or doesn't care?"

"That's something I can't answer," Wade said, shaking his head. "But he'd better wake up soon, or else he'll be flat broke."

Little Bill stared out through the open doorway. Small dust devils were spinning madly in the center of the street and down near Garvey's. The blacksmith pounded on his anvil with ringing regularity.

"Maybe," he said quietly, "just maybe that would be the best thing that could happen to him."

X

They moved out into the brilliant sunlight, came to a sudden stop. Three men were bearing down upon them — Calloway, the mayor, Joe Kingsford, and Wall, the livery stable owner. Their faces were serious and they walked in a determined, pur- poseful way.

"More trouble," Little Bill murmured.

"None we can't handle," Dan said. "Don't let them get under your hide."

"Marshal," Calloway said before he had even come to a halt. "We just ran into that U.S. Marshal . . . Grover, or whatever his name is. He told us your father and his crew of roughnecks are coming in tomorrow, bent on tearing the town up? That true?"

Dan said: "That's what he told me. I saw him this morning."

Kingsford's eyes had noticed the star on Wade's breast. A sort of relief passed over his features. "Looks like we got us a deputy, Mayor," he said.

Calloway and Wall both took a second look. The mayor said: "Fine, fine. I've felt like we've needed a good man for a long time. But about tomorrow . . . what are you planning on doing?"

"Not much I can do, unless Pa breaks a law of some sort."

"Tearing up the town, wrecking property, fighting and scaring people half to death . . . that ain't law breaking?" Wall demanded. "Must be some kind of a law against it."

"There is," Calloway said. "And it's got to be enforced, Marshal. We can't let that Double K crowd take over things with that shipment of money coming in. Now we think you. . . ."

"Just a minute," Dan broke in quietly. "There's a little something I'd like to say. You want law and order in your town. You've hired the marshal, here, and me to get it. All right, suppose you go on about your business and let us do it. Interfering isn't going to help us one bit."

"What's that?" Calloway said sharply.

"I said that, if you will keep out of it, leave the law to us, we'll take care of things. If we have to climb over you every time we turn around, it will just make things tougher."

A slow smile broke across Kingsford's face. Calloway and Herman Wall simply stared. Finally the mayor found his voice.

"Now see here . . . we're responsible to the people. . . ."

"And we're responsible for the law. If Big Bill Krask or any of his boys get out of line tomorrow, they'll damned quick find themselves in a cell. It's as simple as that. Now, gentlemen, if you'll excuse us, we have work to do."

Wade stepped around the three

men and started on down the street. Little Bill, momentarily startled by it all, grinned faintly, nodded to the merchants, and then followed. When they reached the first stop, the Great Western Hotel, Calloway and the other two men still stood where they had left them, talking among themselves.

"I think you sort of set the mayor back on his heels," the young lawman said as they entered the lobby of the hotel. "Nobody around here ever talked to him like that."

"Then I expect it was high time," Wade said. "A man like him means well, but he just gets in the road."

"You mean what you said about Pa?"

"About locking him up? Sure. He breaks the law, he goes to jail to cool off. That's all there is to it."

Little Bill wagged his head doubtfully. "It might turn out to be quite a chore, keeping him there. The crew will make a try to get him out."

"We'll skin that cat when the time comes," Dan said, halting before the hotel's desk. "I want to see your register," he said to the clerk. "I'm interested in anybody that's new in town."

The clerk grinned, ran a hand over his sleek, glossy hair. "Only two strangers, deputy. You and that U.S. marshal."

Further search around Burnt Springs that afternoon failed to turn up any other newcomers, but later that night, in the Rainbow, they discovered two riders, both of whom were familiar to Dan Wade.

"Harley Biggs and Clint Apple-white," he said, pointing the pair out to Krask. "They've been in jail more of the last ten years than they've been outside. I'd like to know what they're doing here." He began to make his way through the crowd to the table where the men sat.

Both glanced up at the approach of the lawmen. Only Applewhite registered surprise at the star on Dan Wade's vest.

"You boys are a little off your regular trail," Dan said, halting before them. "Why?"

"You're a bit off the trail, too, ain't you?" Applewhite said. "Never figured you for a badge-toter."

"Times change," Dan said dryly. "What are you doing around here?"

Biggs shrugged, slouched back into

his chair. "Just passing through. Is there a law against that?"

"Passing through, no . . . staying overnight, yes. How soon will you be riding on?"

The Rainbow's piano dribbled into silence. The steady flow of talk began to fade, dropped to a whisper as the crowd became aware of the conversation between the two lawmen and the strangers.

"Can't say as we're ridin' on tonight," Biggs drawled. "You got some objections to us stayin'?"

Wade said — "Yes." — in a flat, uncompromising voice. "Finish up that whiskey and move on. If I find you around here thirty minutes from now, you'll spend a couple of days in the jug."

"Here! Wait a minute!" the bartender said, pushing through the crowd. "You got no call to be running off my customers like that!"

"I have these two," Dan said.

"Why? They've done nothing!"

"And they won't be getting the chance," Dan replied coolly. He glanced at the two drifters. "All right, pull out."

"I tell you, you can't do this!" the bartender protested, his voice rising to a shrill bleat. "It ain't right, busting in on a man's business this way. I'll go to the mayor!"

"You do that," Dan said, shouldering the sweating man aide. He stepped back, watching Biggs and Applewhite start for the door.

"Remember . . . thirty minutes," he warned.

Biggs shook his head. "Don't go

workin' up a head of steam, Deputy. We'll be long gone by then. No cause for us to hang around this flea-bit town."

The bartender was trembling with rage. "I won't stand for you hurrah-in' my customers like this. . . ."

"You get any more like them tonight or tomorrow, do them a favor and tell them to keep moving. This town is going to be unhealthy for their kind."

He swung about, faced the crowd, scanned it quickly. He saw no one he recognized. He glanced at Little Bill. "Do you know all of these people? Do they all belong around here?"

The marshal swept the patrons of the Rainbow with a critical eye. "No strangers," he said after a moment.

"Good. Let's take a look in the Texas Star. And I want to be sure

Biggs and Applewhite kept going."

The crowd began to drift away, return to their tables or to their places at the bar. The piano struck up again. A gaudily dressed woman, one of the saloons regulars, sauntered toward Little Bill, her lined, painted face drawn into a hard smile.

"First time I remember seeing you in here, Marshal. Where you been keeping yourself?"

"Got a job to take care of," the lawman said stiffly.

"And a Sunday school goer for a wife, too, I hear tell. You're sure not much like your pa! Now, there's a real humdinger of a man. When he takes a hold of a woman. . . ."

Little Bill's arm lashed out, slapped the woman smartly across the mouth.

"Shut up!" he snarled. "You're not

fit to talk about my pa!"

The saloon girl fell back a step, came up against the end of the bar. She touched her bruised lips gingerly, stared at young Krask. Then: "We'll see about that. We'll just see what he's got to say."

Little Bill swung on his heel, started for the batwing doors. Dan glanced at the girl, studied her for several moments.

"Do us all a favor," he said, "forget this. Don't mention it to Big Bill. There's trouble enough brewing."

Her dark eyes snapped angrily. "Trouble? Deputy, you don't know what trouble is. When I get through telling Big Bill what's what, he'll be ready to hang that kid from the nearest cottonwood."

Dan Wade said nothing when he

rejoined the marshal who awaited him on the porch of the Rainbow. There was little point to it now; the damage had been done. More fuel would be heaped upon the fire that raged within Big Bill Krask and his consequent reaction could be only speculation at that point.

They made the rounds of town once more before midnight, and then called it a day. Little Bill went on home to Hannah while Dan headed for the quiet loneliness of his hot, shabby room in the Great Western. He had no illusions as to what faced him and the young marshal that coming day. Not only was there the responsibility of the gold shipment, but there was small doubt Big Bill would be at his worst. The tale the saloon girl would tell him would double his enmity and he would consider the whole affair as a personal affront and insult. Dan groaned inwardly as he walked slowly down the dusty, dark street. How did he manage to get himself into such a situation? And worst of all it meant he was taking sides with a friend — against another friend. He thought of Amos Kincaid's question. Where would he stand when the shooting started? He shook his head, tried to side-step the problem, but there was no ignoring it. The saloon girl had been right, he thought, as he entered his room; the real trouble was yet to come.

XI

The stage carrying the shipment of gold and currency whirled into Burnt

Springs shortly after 5:00 the next afternoon. It arrived ahead of the soldiers from Fort Glade who had not yet put in an appearance. Dan Wade, standing at the corner of Kingsford's store, watched it roll up to the bank and slide to a halt in a boil of dust.

A little farther along Little Bill Krask, shotgun in hand, had taken up a position in front of the Texas Star. Almost directly opposite him across the street, Luke Grover, his frock coat brushed back to reveal not one but two revolvers, leaned against the corner of the Chicago Café. As the stage halted in its pall of yellow powder, Dan and Krask moved in closer. The guard, sitting beside the driver, spat, looked down at Little Bill.

"Where's the soldiers?"

"You can see they're not here yet," Grover snapped before the lawman could reply. "Hurry it up. Get that money unloaded from this hack and inside."

The driver spat again, studied the government man thoughtfully. To Little Bill he said: "Just who the hell is he?"

"A U.S. marshal, Pete," Krask replied. "Sent down here to look after the shipment. They got rumors of a hold-up."

"So?" the guard exclaimed. He leaned down, slapped hard against the side of the coach. "All right, boys, unload. Soldiers ain't here, so it goes into the bank this time."

A chain rattled within the vehicle. The door swung open. Two men supporting a small, ironbound chest between them stepped into the street. In their free hands they carried cocked revolvers.

"Hurry it up!" Grover urged, repeating himself.

"Keep your shirt on," one of the guards muttered. "Goin' as fast as we can."

Dan wheeled slowly around, made a complete and thorough survey of the street and of all the buildings that stood along its edges. Two men slouched on the porch that fronted the Rainbow. A woman and a half-grown child had paused near Hotchkiss's store to watch. Otherwise Burnt Springs appeared deserted and he could see nothing suspicious or out of the ordinary.

The men carrying the money,

backed now by Pete who had climbed down from the box, reached the door of the bank and entered. Grover followed to that point, halted as if to bar it to anyone else who might seek to go inside.

"Where's those damn' soldiers?" he demanded peevishly. "This is one time they ought to be here."

Little Bill shook his head. "I doubt if they'll make it today. They're usually here by noon or a bit after if they're going to be early. They'll probably show up in the morning now."

"Stinking luck," Grover said. "It means we'll have to stand a night watch."

The guards came through the doorway at that moment, their chore completed. The government man looked them up and down.

"How about sticking around until the Army comes? We could use a little help."

Pete bit a fresh chunk of tobacco off the plug he carried. "Nope, not us. We got business waitin' for us somewhere else. What'd you say your name was, Marshal?"

"Don't remember telling you, but it's Grover, Luke Grover. Why?"

"Nothin' much. Just figured it was sort of funny we didn't hear nothin' about you bein' here."

Grover shrugged. "Nothing funny about it. I'm straight out of the head office. We don't think it's necessary to tell every jerk-water way-station driver and shotgun messenger our business."

Pete grinned. "Man asks a question,

he gets a answer. Ain't always a civil one but it's a answer. *Adiós*, Marshal . . . see you in church."

He swung up beside the driver. The other two men were already inside the coach. The driver popped his whip and the four-up lunged forward in the harness, surged out into the street in a tight circle. A moment later the coach was only a swirl of dust racing southward.

Luke Grover stood motionlessly, his gaze on the vanishing cloud. "Before I leave here," he said slowly, "I want the names of those four men. They're going into my report. No good reason why they couldn't have delayed overnight and given us some help."

Dan Wade was thinking of the guard's remark. It seemed strange to him also that the stage authorities had not known about Luke Grover, that, in this instance at least, they had not instructed the guards and driver to give the lawman all the co-operation he needed. On the other hand, Grover's blunt explanation could have been the exact truth. And possibly it could have been a case of having no time in which to make advance preparations.

"You could have ordered them to wait over," he said then. "Expect your authority would have covered that, being a federal man."

"Guess I could've," Grover said thoughtfully. "Don't know why I didn't think of it. But no use hashing over it now," he added, rubbing his hands together. "Too late to call them back. We've got to make plans for the night. Since the Army's not likely to show up until morning, we've got no choice but to stand guard until then. Agree?"

"Whatever you say," Little Bill replied. "I don't think there's much danger, however, with the money locked in the vault."

"Taking no chances on it," Grover said. "And I sure won't rest easy until the soldiers take over and I hand the shipment to Major Ives at the fort."

"You going back with them?" Dan asked.

"Yes, sir. My job is to see that money through right up to the moment it's put into Ives's safe at Fort Glade. My responsibility ends there, not before."

Dan said: "I understand. With them being so careful it's a wonder they didn't put you on as a sort of shotgun messenger right at the start, have you ride with the shipment from the beginning."

"About the only reason they didn't was because there wasn't time," the lawman said. "Anyway, this is where we expected the trouble."

Little Bill said: "Let's hope none comes. How do we work this? No sense in all three of us standing here in front of the bank."

"True," Grover said crisply. "I was about to suggest to you, Marshal, that one of you stay here, the other go around back. I'll just drift around town, keep my eyes peeled and my ears open for anybody or anything suspicious. That way we'll be covering everything."

Krask glanced at Dan. "Sound good to you?"

Wade nodded. "Good a plan as any."

"You think of something better?" Grover asked, almost belligerently.

"No," Dan drawled. "Like I said, it's as good a plan as any. You take the back," he said, turning to Little Bill. "Anybody shows up you don't know is all right, sing out."

The young marshal nodded, swung off toward the rear of the structure. Dan's motive reached further than the reason implied; it was just as well Little Bill be out of sight when his pa rode into town. The longer the meeting between them was delayed, the better for all concerned.

"I'll be close by," Grover said, adjusting the position of his crossed gun belts. "You want me, yell."

"I figure on it," Dan said. "But this

responsibility is as much yours as ours. Don't get too far away and keep out of places where you can't hear me."

"Don't worry about that," the federal man said, "I've been through. . . ."

He checked his words abruptly. A spatter of gunshots and the hard pounding of running horses broke across the hot evening air. The racket came from beyond Garvey's. Yells lifted and another round of shooting sounded. A half a dozen or more riders swept around the corner of the Great Western, came racing down the street.

Dan Wade swore softly. Big Bill Krask and his Double K hardcases had arrived.

XII

Dan shuttered a glance at Grover. A hard smile pulled at the lawman's lips briefly, then faded. Along the side of the bank the rap of Little Bill coming up at a run could be heard. Wade lifted his arm, waved the lawman back.

"Just the Double K bunch," he said. "Stay in the alley."

He listened, hopeful Krask would accept his explanation and return to his post. A moment later he breathed easier. Little Bill had obeyed. He brought his attention back to the street. The cattleman and his riders had halted before the Rainbow, were dismounting. They had holstered their pistols, more interested at that moment, apparently, in slaking their thirst. Two of the men gathered up the reins of the horses, led them off toward Garvey's. The remainder followed Big Bill across the gallery and through the batwing doors into the saloon.

A great shout of welcome and laughter greeted the rancher and his crew. Most likely the elder Krask was a generous spender, and, while he was present, he doubtless stood for all drinks.

Grover hitched at his guns again. "I expect it would be smart to head on down that way, keep an eye on things."

"Do me a favor," Dan said. "Tell Big Bill I want him and his men to stay inside the Rainbow. They get out on the street, causing trouble, I'm locking them up."

"I'll tell him," Grover said. "You want me, just holler."

Dan watched the lawman strike off through the dust. He was an odd sort; he professed a strong interest in the need for precautions, yet was doing little himself to protect the money. Dan guessed Grover knew what he was about, but for his own self, if he were worried about the shipment, he would at that moment be either inside the bank with a shotgun across his knees, or atop the building directly across the street where he could see everything that moved. A thought moved into Dan's mind. Could it be the danger of a hold-up was far less than the government man indicated, that it was merely a plan to arouse the town, to jar it to wakefulness, and make it more aware of its responsibility? It was possible — but it was Luke Grover's affair; he knew what he was doing. Dan brushed it all away, glanced toward the rear of the bank building.

"Everything all right back there?"

"All set," Little Bill replied. "You getting hungry?"

"No, a little early for me."

"Ought to have told Hannah. She could have fixed us up a basket of fried chicken."

"Taste mighty good," Dan admitted.

He had brought his attention back to the Rainbow. Luke Grover, following an erratic, vagrant course down the street, in and out of the passageways, appeared on the gallery fronting the saloon. He paused there for a short time, his eyes turned toward the east road; abruptly he wheeled, pushed through the swinging doors into the blare of light and noise.

An hour wore by, two. . . . Big Bill and his men were still in the saloon fortifying themselves well with whiskey, Dan assumed. He hoped Grover had passed along his warning but there was little likelihood the rancher would heed it. Big Bill was the sort who took orders from no one. And this night, he had served notice, was to be one of particular importance. There was one encouraging possibility; Luke Grover also was in the Rainbow. Perhaps he could compel Krask and his crew to stay in line.

A figure broke suddenly from the wall of darkness beyond Kingsford's.

Dan came to quick attention. A moment later he saw it was a woman, her dress ghostly white in the deep shadows. He relaxed, leaned back against the wall of the bank, watched her easy, graceful approach. It was Hannah.

When she reached the center of the street, she hesitated, called softly: "Bill?"

"Over here, ma'am," Dan said, replying.

She came on at the sound of his voice. "Oh, it's you, Dan. I brought you and Bill some supper. One of our neighbors told me what you were doing."

"Bill's around back," Wade said. "And I'm obliged to you for thinking of us. Not much chance of us getting away for a bite to eat."

She removed a plate from the basket she carried, handed it to him. It was piled high with fried chicken and still warm biscuits.

"I'll take the rest to Bill," she said. "If you would like coffee, I can get it from the café."

"This will do fine," Dan murmured. The chicken was crisp and delicious, as were the biscuits. Dan had not realized he was so hungry until it dawned upon him he had again skipped the noon meal. It was an old trail habit of a solitary rider. Usually he ate a hearty breakfast and a good supper. Halting during the noon hour to prepare food when he was on the move never occurred to him. And now, when he was within the circle of civilization, it was hard to break the pattern.

There was a shout down in front of the Rainbow. Dan threw his attention to that point. A half dozen men were on the porch, more were crowding through the doors. All were watching two cowboys, locked in each others arms as they wrestled about in the dust. Both went over, prone into the street. The smaller of the two sprang clear. He drew back his booted foot, lashed out at the other. The blow caught the man on the chin. His head snapped to the side. He hung momentarily and then fell forward, burying his face in the ankle-deep dust.

A new burst of yells went up. Several men pushed forward to slap the victor on the back. A few turned, headed back into the saloon; others came out. Dan watched narrowly.

This could be the beginning, the springboard that would launch the violence he felt so certain was bound to come.

He heard the whisper of Hannah's flowing dress behind him, caught the fresh, clean smell of her perfume.

"Would you like for me to get that coffee now, Dan?" she asked, pausing at his shoulder. "I'm going after a cup for Bill."

Wade, his gaze now riveted to four men down the street, shook his head. "Best we forget it," he said, handing her his empty plate. "Obliged just the same."

"But I'm getting it for Bill. . . ."

The four men had moved away from the Rainbow, were advancing slowly along the street.

"Forget it," Dan said again. "Get

away from here, Hannah. Go home . . . please."

She followed his rigid line of vision. A moment later she was running lightly toward Kingsford's, hurrying off into the darkness for the safety of her home.

"Something wrong?" Little Bill called from the rear of the bank.

"Visitors coming," Dan replied. "Four of them. Can't make out who they are. Some of the Double K bunch, I'd guess."

"Want me up there?"

"No, hold your place. Let me handle it."

"Where the hell's this Luke Grover?" the lawman wondered, his tone angry and impatient. "Thought he was going to be around, helping out."

"Last I saw of him he was going

into the Rainbow," Dan said. "I was hoping he'd make your pa and his crowd stay inside. I guess he couldn't do it. No more talking, now. I'd as soon nobody knows where you are."

He watched the quartet draw up closer. They passed through a shaft of light that flared from a window of the Great Western. He recognized all four: Cully, Levi Ferrel, Carl Jackson, and the foreman, Ross Oliver. He allowed them to draw up within a dozen paces.

"Far enough!" he barked suddenly, showing himself.

They came to a quick halt. Levi, caught off balance, stumbled against the redhead, cursing fluently.

"What do you want?" Wade demanded.

There was a moment's pause, then

Oliver said: "You. Old Cully here's got a score to settle with you. We aim to see he gets the chance."

Dan said: "Later. Come around tomorrow. Right now I got other things to do."

"You ain't that busy," Oliver said, his voice thick.

"Too busy to fool with you," Wade said. "Now, head on back to the saloon or I'll lock you up."

"You'll lock us up?" It was Cully. "Since when did you get to be marshal?"

"He's sure wearin' a star," Levi said. "Maybe we got us a new lawman."

"Don't make any difference," Oliver said. "We come here to help Cully. Spread out. Work in from all sides. The thing to do is grab him, hold him so's Cully. . . ."

"Don't try it," Dan warned. "First man that does, gets a bullet."

Oliver laughed. "Don't let him bluff you, boys. He can't shoot us all . . . and he's by himself."

"Not quite," Little Bill's voice broke from the darkness along the bank.

The four men froze. Levi said: "Why, that's our reg'lar marshal! Your pa's lookin' for you, kid."

"He knows where to find me," Krask said.

"Your wife know you're out here in the dark?" Oliver asked in the same bantering tone. "Young 'uns ain't supposed to be running loose this time of night."

"Move on," Dan Wade said, his words sharp. "We don't want trouble with you . . . not tonight."

"What's wrong with tonight?"

"You heard what he said," Little Bill broke in. "Get off the street . . . now!"

"You listening, boys?" Oliver said. "You better hark to what the marshal's telling you. He's real fierce."

There was a loud, metallic click in the deep shadows. It was followed immediately by a second, identical sound.

"That was the hammers on a double-barreled shotgun," the young lawman said. "It's pointed straight at your bellies. Any of you takes one step except back toward the Rainbow, I'll scatter him all over the street."

Ross Oliver had no answer to that for there was no mistaking the promise in Krask's tone. Levi wheeled carefully around.

"Come on," he said, "let's be gettin' back to the saloon. Ought to tell the old man where his kid is, anyway."

"I ain't finished my business with this smart Aleck jasper yet," Cully said, protesting mildly.

"You won't have much fun doing it with your guts strung all over hell," Oliver said scornfully. "We've got plenty of time."

They turned about, trooped off down the street.

Little Bill sighed audibly. "Close," he said. "Figured we were in for it there for a few minutes."

"We are now for sure," Dan said grimly. "Long as your pa didn't know exactly where you were, we had no problem."

He watched Oliver and the others mount the two steps to the Rainbow's porch, making their way across it and disappearing into the building. In only moments they were back, now with several other men. There was no mistaking the huge figure in the lead — Big Bill Krask.

"Here he comes," Wade said. "This is going to be a little rough, especially for you. Good chance for you to duck out if you've got the notion."

There was a long silence while Little Bill considered. Then, in a low voice, he said: "No. I reckon it might as well be here, tonight, as anywhere else."

XIII

They paused in the intersection of Burnt Spring's two streets, immediately in front of the Rainbow. In the light that streamed from the saloon

Dan could distinguish Big Bill, Oliver, and several more of the Double K crew. Another dozen women and men had bailed out of the Rainbow, swelling the crowd, their voices adding to the hubbub.

After several minutes the knot of people began to flow down the dusty avenue, aiming for the bank. Four men were distinctly in the lead now: Krask, Ross Oliver, Cully, and Levi. Dan watched them draw nearer, feeling the tension rise as a deep quiet settled over the town.

"Better let me handle this!" he called to Little Bill. "Maybe I can talk your pa out of it."

Again the young marshal was silent as he thought over the suggestion. And again he declined. "No. It's my quarrel, not yours."

Dan had a momentary wish that Hannah could be somewhere close by, that she might see and realize the hour had finally come when her husband was facing up to his problem. But he quickly amended that hope. The incident could turn into a tragic affair, one better not witnessed by the girl. Hannah Krask could be proud of her man now, even as Dan Wade felt a strong lift within himself for the young marshal.

The crowd slowed as it reached the front of the hotel. Big Bill said something about another drink. A bottle was passed to him. He took a long swallow and once more they came on. Dan moved away from the dark shadows along the bank building, took a long stride deeper into the street. A dozen yards away Big Bill saw him, halted.

"That you, lawman?"

The cattleman had not called his son by name, or even recognized a relationship. He was keeping that out of his mind, stubbornly maintaining a separation of identities.

"No, it's me . . . Dan Wade."

Ross Oliver leaned toward Krask, said something to him. The rancher pushed forward another unsteady step.

"Close enough!" Dan said in a flat, warning tone.

Big Bill halted. "You taking sides with that tin star, boy? You forgetting who's your friend?"

Dan said: "No, I'm just trying to keep you from making a mistake. It's your own son, your own flesh and blood you're after."

"No son of mine. He walked out on me."

"You forced his hand. Any man has the right to choose his own life."

Ross Oliver again turned to Krask, said something to him in a quick, angry way.

"You're listening to the wrong man there," Dan said. "He's stealing you blind . . . and he's prodding this trouble between you and Little Bill. If you'd sober up for a day and take a good look around. . . ."

"Ross's all right!" Big Bill shouted, staggering a little. "He's doing what I tell him!"

"You sure? You know how many cows you got left on the range?"

"Ain't nobody's business but mine!" the elder Krask yelled. "Where's that kid . . . that tin star?

Why ain't he here talking for himself?"

From the darkness beyond Wade, Little Bill said: "I'm here, Pa."

The rancher stiffened. "Hiding, eh? Come on out where I can see you."

Dan heard the thud of the lawman's heels as he moved up from his position. He threw a hard look at the crowd. Where the devil was Luke Grover? He should be there, doing his part to protect the shipment. It was risky to leave the rear of the bank unguarded. If there were outlaws lurking about now would be an ideal time for them to make their try. Everyone's attention was on the trouble in the street.

Little Bill came to a halt an arm's length to the right of Dan. "I wasn't hiding," he said calmly. "I've got a job to do and I'm trying to do it."

"I put him there," Wade said. "I was hoping I could keep you two apart but your friends spoiled that. If you didn't have such a thick head, you'd see I'm right."

"Right about what, boy?"

"That they want this trouble between you and Little Bill. They want you dead. Then they'd own everything you got. They're out to get rid of you, one way or another."

Oliver lurched forward. "That's a damn' lie!"

Dan Wade's gun was in his hand in a swift blur of motion. "Don't try it, Ross! For what you've done to Big Bill, I'd like a reason to kill you!"

The foreman halted abruptly. Krask reached out, grasped him by the shoulder, and drew him back roughly.

"Keep out of this!" he snarled. "Both of you . . . all of you! Keep your noses out of my doings. This is betwixt me and that tin star."

Little Bill said: "Forget it, Pa. Go on home. I won't fight you."

"Well, you're going to whether you want to or not! I'm going to tear that badge off you and give you the beating of your life. You got a lesson coming. You've been doing a lot of talking about me and you've been slapping my friends around, insulting them and making out like you were a real big man. Now you're going to answer to me."

"Forget it. . . ."

"And there's a few others around here that's been shooting off their mouths. I figure they got a lesson coming, too. Soon as I'm done with you, I'm starting on them . . . me and my boys. This town's going to be sorry for what it's been saying . . . what's left of it when I'm done."

"You're drunk, Pa. Mount up and go home."

"Don't be ordering me around! You ready to step out here and face me or are you running again?"

"I'm not afraid of you," Little Bill said quietly. "Not in the way you think. Guess I never was. It was only that I wanted to dodge trouble."

"You ain't dodging no more. And I'm through jawing with you."

"What you goin' to use on him, Bill?" a voice from the crowd yelled. "A willow switch?"

Big Bill whirled around. "Switch, hell! He fancies himself with a six-gun. I aim to show him what a real hand with an iron looks like!"

An instant hush fell over the street. It was as if the persons gathered there, having goaded their man to the point of culmination all in the spirit of great fun, were startled to discover it was not great fun after all, was instead a serious and deadly situation.

"You hear me, lawman?" the rancher shouted. "I was going to use my hands on you, but I've changed my mind. You and me are going to settle things with guns. You want, you better start running now."

"I'm not running . . . and I won't fight you, Pa. Not with a gun or anything else."

"Then you're scared, no more guts than a mangy jack rabbit."

The inevitable Dan Wade had

feared was at hand. The crisis he had hoped would not come, but deep in his heart knew was unavoidable, had shaped up. He took a step to the side, away from Little Bill.

"He's a better man than you'll ever be," he said, throwing the words at Krask. "I always figured you for the best. I was wrong. You're nothing but a big-mouthed drunk . . . a liar!"

The cattleman's head snapped up. "What's that you said? You talking to me, boy?"

"I'm talking to you," Dan said evenly. "And I'll back up everything I said."

"Then me and you's got some business to take care of, just as soon as I'm finished with that tin star."

"No, it's right now. I've got first call."

The sudden, shattering blast of a pistol brought everyone around. Luke Grover, with a half a dozen or so cavalrymen still on the saddle, stood in front of the Chicago Café. They had apparently come up from the south end of the street, completely unnoticed. A sigh of relief slipped through Dan Wade's lips. At least that worry was over. The responsibility for the money shipment no longer rested on his and Little Bill's shoulders.

"I want you all to move away from here," the federal officer said, his voice hard. "I don't intend to meddle in your local affairs, but I've got work to do and I'm taking no chance on interference. If you've got some fighting to do, do it down at the other end of the street."

Dan studied the waiting soldiers, a frown on his face. Something apparently had delayed them and they looked none too happy. He glanced at Grover.

"Are you loading up and pulling out tonight?"

"Why not? Army finally got here. Sooner I get this job over with, better I like it."

"Little risky traveling at night," Little Bill observed.

"Be as hard for outlaws to see us as it is for us to spot them. Works both ways. Anyway, looks like it was all just a rumor." Grover swung his eyes to the crowd. "Well, how about it? You moving on down to the other end of the street or do I call on these soldiers to step in?"

"Just you simmer down a mite," Big

Bill said. "Happens this is my town. Don't go crowding me." He brought his attention back to Dan. "You was shooting off your lip plenty loud a minute ago. You still figure to back it up?"

"Any time you say," Wade replied.

"Ten minutes . . . down in front of the Rainbow," Krask snapped. "I'll be waiting. And you be there, too," he added to Little Bill. "I get this saddle tramp out of the way, I'll be ready for you."

Without waiting for an answer from either man, the cattleman wheeled about and started back for the saloon, the crowd trailing along in his wake.

Immediately the cavalrymen rode in to the hitch rack that served the bank, dismounted. Dan gave them a brief glance — a lieutenant, a sergeant, and four privates. All were tough-appearing, hardened soldiers. Major Ives had chosen a well-experienced crew to escort Grover.

"Where the hell's that banker?" the federal man wondered. "He's supposed to be here and open up for me."

"Somebody's coming now," the lieutenant said. "That him?"

"That's him," Little Bill said. "You finished with us, Marshal?"

"I am . . . and I'm much obliged. Like I said, it appears this hold-up was just talk, but we couldn't see taking any chances. Everything's safe now, with the Army here."

"Hey, drifter!" It was Ross Oliver, shouting from the crowd now gathered in front of the saloon. "We're waitin'!"

Wade nodded to Grover, started off down the street. At his shoulder Little Bill said: "You didn't fool me, Dan, getting yourself crossways with Pa. I won't let you go through with it."

Wade smiled bleakly. "Nothing you can do about it now."

XIV

They walked slowly through the powdery dust. The full import of his situation was registering on Dan Wade's consciousness in those moments, the incredible position of being forced into a gunfight with a friend he had always admired and respected — a man for whom he now felt only sorrow and pity.

"It's my doing," Little Bill murmured. "My own fight. I won't let you stand for me."

"You want to shoot it out with your own pa . . . kill him?"

"He might kill me instead."

"Not likely, not if you tried. You're better with a gun than he is. You know that."

The young lawman was silent. Dan looked ahead. The crowd in front of the Rainbow had multiplied as word of the showdown had spread.

"And he knows it," Little Bill said, taking up the conversation where it had broken off. "Same as he knows he'll be no match for you. What's the matter with him? Why does he keep pressing it?"

Wade paused, glancing back over his shoulder. Luke Grover and the soldiers were just entering the bank building. In a few more minutes they would have the shipment loaded and be on their way.

"Who knows?" he said, replying to the lawman. "Pride and stubbornness, for one thing. And the yapping Ross Oliver and the others have been doing. Mix that up with the liquor he's guzzling and maybe you've got your reason. He can't think straight. If he ever got the chance to sober up, he'd realize what was going on."

"They're the ones we ought to be throwing down on," the lawman said, his voice tight and angry. "Oliver and Cully . . . all the rest. I wouldn't mind taking on the whole bunch."

Dan Wade came to a dead stop. A glimmer of an idea, of hope, slipped into his mind. "Maybe that's the answer," he said, his eyes on the

crowd. "It could be what we're looking for."

Little Bill moved around to where
he could face the tall rider. "Answer
to what?"

"To your pa . . . to straightening
out this mess. Do you mean what you
said, that you're willing to stand up
against Ross Oliver and his bunch?
Odds will be maybe five or six to our
two."

"A shoot-out?"

"It'll probably be just that, unless
I'm figuring Ross Oliver wrong."

"And leave Pa out of it?"

"That's the idea."

"I'm ready," Little Bill said without
hesitation. "What are you figuring to
do?"

"First we find Amos Kincaid," Dan
said. "Then I'll explain."

They moved on down the street into the crowd. Big Bill, standing a bit to one side with Oliver and several of his crew, watched Wade approach with dull interest. He ignored his son.

"You ready, boy?"

Dan shook his head. "Don't rush me. There's a couple of things I have to do."

"You getting cold feet?"

"No," Wade said, glancing over the expectant faces turned toward him. "I want to do this thing up right."

Kincaid was not in the two dozen or so persons gathered in the street. Dan motioned to Little Bill.

"Keep that scatter-gun pointed at Ross and his bunch," he said. "I'm taking a look in the saloon, and I don't fancy a bullet in my back."

The marshal nodded. "I'd like for

one of them to make a wrong move. I figure I owe somebody there for a rap on the head the other night."

Dan shouldered his way across the gallery of the Rainbow and pushed through the doors. The saloon was completely empty. Disturbed, he wheeled about. The old cowpuncher had said definitely he would be in town and Dan knew Kincaid well enough to know he would not fail. Something had happened to keep Kincaid from keeping his promise.

"Quit stallin'," Cully said, as Wade stepped back into the street. "You was talkin' mighty big a few minutes ago. You aim to weasel out now?"

Dan whirled on the man, caught him by the shirt front, jerked him forward. "I'm looking for Amos Kincaid. He was supposed to be here.

You know any reason why he's not?"

Cully's flushed face paled. His eyes flared, then squeezed down to small slits. "How the hell would I know where he is?"

"He said he'd be here. And he told me you'd jumped him before."

"He's got a long nose . . . ," the redhead blurted, and stopped suddenly.

Anger rocked through Dan Wade. His free hand lashed out, slapped Cully hard across the face. "If you've laid a finger on that old man. . . ."

"What's going on here?" Big Bill demanded, shoving up behind the redhead. "What you hurrahing him for? It's you and me that's got things to settle."

"He's backin' down," Ross Oliver declared in a loud voice. "That's

what he's doin'. Trying to start some-
thin' with somebody else so's he
won't have to face you."

"Let me have him!" Cully yelled,
beside himself with rage. "Been wantin' my chance with this jasper. . . .'"

"Shut up," Big Bill said. "He'd blow
your head off before you knew what
was going on." The rancher peered at
Dan. "You backing down from me?
Is that what this's all about?"

"You know better. I'm trying to find
out what's happened to Amos Kincaid. I've got a hunch he's been hurt,
or maybe he's dead."

"Amos?" the cattleman echoed, his
voice cracking a little. "Who'd be
wanting to hurt him?"

"Any of that bunch you call a crew.
The redhead there beat him up once
before . . . just because he was trying

to look out for you."

Big Bill frowned. "Old Amos? Never heard nothing about it. Anyway, it's got nothing to do with us. I'm waiting, boy, waiting for you to get out there in the street."

"He ain't got the guts," Ross Oliver murmured, a sly grin on his face.

Dan studied the foreman's ruddy face. "Maybe you'd like to try first. It'd be a good way for me to limber up my arm."

Oliver's grin faded. "I ain't hornin' in on the boss' fun," he said, shrugging. "You're his meat."

"And you're mine," Dan said. "Remember that, Ross. I'm coming for you when this is finished."

"I'll be ready," Oliver said, and winked broadly at Cully and the others.

Dan turned about. Directly before him he saw Joe Kingsford. He motioned to the merchant, drew him off to one side. He caught Little Bill's attention, waved him over.

"Fixin' up your funeral?" Levi called. "Don't worry none about it. We'll see you're planted . . . good and deep."

The crowd roared with laughter. Cully said something else and there was another burst. Dan faced the merchant.

"Joe, we need your help. I don't want this shoot-out to go through."

"If you don't stand up to him, everybody will think you're backing down."

"It makes no difference what they think. I'm not going out there and kill Big Bill and I sure don't aim to let him kill me."

"What can I do about it?"

"Get Big Bill inside the Rainbow, away from that crowd. I don't care how you handle it . . . just so you do it."

"I've got to have some kind of reason."

Wade nodded. "I'll furnish it. The important thing is to get him away from Oliver and his bunch. Little Bill and I have some business with them that needs taking care of."

Light broke across Kingsford's features. "You two taking them on? All of them?"

Dan said: "Big Bill's in a fog. He doesn't know what's going on, they've got him that fuddled. Once we get them out of the picture, I think we can bring him to his senses."

"A hard bunch," the merchant said doubtfully. "Could be you're biting off a big chew."

"We'll take our chances," the lawman said.

The crowd was growing noisier, egged on by Oliver and his followers. Shouts for Wade to stand and draw or ride out of town, a branded coward, echoed along the street.

Dan glanced at Kingsford, at Little Bill. "We all set?"

"You call the turn," the younger Krask replied, handing the shotgun to Kingsford. "Hold this, Joe. I won't be using it."

Kingsford accepted the weapon, hung it in the crook of his arm. "All you want me to do is get Big Bill out of the crowd and into the saloon."

"That's it," Dan said. "I don't trust

Oliver and his bunch. One way or another they're going to get a bullet into him. If not by me, by one of them."

"I see. All right, I'll work it somehow. You start things off."

Dan wheeled. He glanced at Big Bill Krask, flanked closely by the Double K crew. "Keep an eye on Oliver and the others," he said in a low voice to the young lawman. "Don't make a move until your pa is out of the way."

He took a step toward the center of the street, halted abruptly, his eyes reaching beyond the crowd. A riderless horse had walked into the light, a small, chunky buckskin wearing a McClellan Army saddle and a bold U.S. brand on its hip.

XV

All the small, tag ends of doubt that had been plaguing Dan Wade suddenly fused, crystallized in his mind. He knew now what it was that had disturbed him, had given life to the vague worry that had beset him as he watched the squad of soldiers from Fort Glade ride in and dismount before the bank. The horses did not wear Army brands — and the men forked stock saddles, not the conventional government issue. Major Ives, a spit and polish officer who went strictly by the book, would never permit such disregard of regulations. Somewhere between the Army post and the settlement an ambush had taken place. The killers had appropriated the cavalrymen's uniforms, but apparently had not bothered to acquire their horses also; one of the straying Army mounts had managed to find his way into town.

Wade threw a hurried look down the street. Grover and the imposters were still there. They were ready to pull out. Two had mounted; others were swinging up. The federal man was saying something to Dawson, the banker.

"Outlaws!" Dan suddenly yelled. "It's a hold-up! Those men aren't soldiers! Come on," he added to Little Bill, and started for the bank at a run. "We've got to warn Grover . . . help him!"

"Hey!" the elder Krask's voice thundered along the buildings. "What's going on? Where do you think . . . ?"

"He's runnin'!" Cully shouted. "By God, he's runnin' out on the fight!"

"Head him off! Cut him down!" It was Ross Oliver's voice. "Don't let him get away!"

Wade half turned in stride, the foreman's words sending a stream of warning through him. He saw Cully and Levi bolt from the crowd, saw them dragging out their guns. He drew fast, snapped a shot at the redhead. Cully went to his knees as the bullet smashed into him. Levi halted uncertainly. Farther back Dan could see Kingsford clutching Big Bill Krask's arm, talking to him earnestly. Evidently the merchant thought this was the diversion he had been promised.

There was no time to stop, even to call back an explanation to the now jeering crowd. He glanced ahead, to the bank. Grover was walking to his horse, his face turned toward the street.

"Marshal . . . it's a hold-up!" Little Bill cried. "Those men aren't soldiers . . . they're outlaws!"

Grover either didn't hear or understand. He placed his foot in the stirrup, gained the saddle. The horses beyond him began to mill about.

"Watch them!" Dan yelled his warning to Little Bill, a dozen paces to his right. "They'll open up at us any second!"

"I'm ready," the lawman said grimly.

Something was happening back in front of the Rainbow. Dan could hear the confused babble of voices, of shouts. He did not look around. It could be that Oliver and the rest of the crew were following, were coming to claim vengeance for his shooting down Cully. He grinned bleakly; if so, they'd have to wait their turn.

The bank was just ahead. Dan put his attention on the government man. "Grover . . . those soldiers are fakes . . . they're outlaws! Can't you hear me?"

Luke Grover wheeled his horse about. He looked straight at Dan and Little Bill. "I hear you," he said, and drew his pistol.

Dan heard the crack of the weapon, saw the orange circle of its powder flash. He felt the breath of the bullet as it skimmed his cheek — and only then realized what it meant. Grover was no U.S. marshal — he was an outlaw! "Hit the dirt!" he howled at

Little Bill as he saw Grover's gun flame again.

He went into the ankle-deep dust, began to roll. He fired as he came onto his belly, aimed at the first and nearest target. It was one of the bogus soldiers. The man jolted from the impact of the slug, started to fall.

Little Bill opened up at that moment. The riders in front of the bank were wheeling uncertainly. A second outlaw was down, lying partly on the ground with one foot still caught in the stirrup of his saddle. Little Bill had scored, too.

A sudden hail of bullets erupted from Grover and the others. Dust spurted up around Dan, showering him with fine, dry powder. He heard the young lawman gasp, knew instantly he had been hit.

He sent an answering fire at the outlaws, a wild, sudden rage possessing him. A third rider sagged, but did not fall. Dan threw an anxious look at Little Bill. The lawman was not shooting, simply laying full length in the center of the street. He had been hit hard, possibly was dead.

Dan's pistol clicked as a spent cartridge came up. He cursed, rolled to his back. He hastily thumbed a half dozen bullets from his belt loops, punched out the empties, and shoved the fresh loads into the cylinder. He heard the hard thud of horses' hoofs, glanced up. Grover and the three men able to ride were swerving toward him. Their guns began to blaze.

He snapped the loading gate of his .44 shut, rolling frantically to one side. He had to escape not only the murderous rain of bullets they were throwing at him as they sought to break through and reach the open ground behind him, but the oncoming horses as well. He fired hastily, taking no aim, hoping only to halt the charge. A slug drove into one of the horses, dropped him to his knees. The outlaw leaped from the saddle, struck on his head and one shoulder.

Dan saw Grover in that moment, only a dozen yards away. He twisted about for a shot, heard Little Bill's revolver blast again. Hope surged through him. The lawman was still alive. Wade leveled on Grover, saw another of the outlaws wheel straight for the wounded Krask. He prayed Little Bill was aware of the man's close presence. He saw Grover throw himself to one side, knew he had missed his shot the instant he squeezed the trigger.

"Your last try!" the false marshal yelled, his lips pulled back into a hard grin.

Wade struggled to get up, to roll to his feet, throw himself from the path of the horse. Grover was too near. Dan saw the sudden, looming shape of the outlaw's mount before him, heard the deafening crash of Grover's gun almost against his head.

In the fragment of time he felt the shocking wallop of the horse's body against him, he went backward and down into the dust, rolling over and over. Grover's voice again touched him.

"So long cowboy!"

The outlaw would kill him now; he would have an easy chore. His own gun was empty; he was flat in the street, half dazed from the collision with the running horse.

The town echoed with the blast of a shotgun, two thunderous reports. The rapid crack of a pistol followed immediately. Dan pulled himself about. Grover's horse, with no rider on the saddle, was trotting off toward the other loose animals. He sat up, his mind clearing rapidly now. Two men were upright. Joe Kingsford, carrying the shotgun the marshal had thrust upon him, and Big Bill Krask, a smoking pistol in his hand.

The cattleman moved to where his son lay. Dan watched him drop hesitantly to his knees, pause momentarily, and then reach down and gather the boy into his arms. The crowd that had trailed up from the front of the Rainbow fell silent.

"You all right?" Kingsford called to Dan through the pall of dust.

"I'll make it," Dan said. "I was lucky." He remained where he sat, finishing the chore of reloading his gun.

"That damn' Grover . . . ," Kingsford muttered. "Sure had me fooled. Looks like Little Bill's hurt bad." He turned away, started for the cattleman and his son.

Dan flung a glance at the pair. Big Bill was still on his knees. He was holding the young marshal against his chest.

"Let them be," Dan said, rising to his feet. "This is the time they both need. Somebody go after the doc?"

"Reckon you're right," the merchant said. "Yeah, Doc's on his way."

Dan walked to where Luke Grover lay. The man was dead. He had taken a charge from Kingsford's shotgun. Methodically the deputy went on to each of the other outlaws. Two were still alive. But the man Big Bill had stopped just as he was swinging in to finish off the young marshal was not one of those; the cattleman's bullet had struck him squarely between the eyes. Big Bill was still expert with a six-gun.

"Let me in here."

Dan heard the doctor's words, gentle, but firm, as he dropped beside the Krasks. George Calloway came up at a trot, glanced around briefly, and then hurried to where Dan and Kingsford stood. The crowd had pulled in closer, now formed an almost complete ring in the street.

"Don't quite understand all this," Calloway said. "You mean Grover wasn't a U.S. marshal at all? And those soldiers weren't soldiers?"

Dan nodded. "Somewhere there's a genuine marshal lying dead, I expect. Grover had to get the badge and papers somewhere. We ought to send word to Major Ives. Could be they'll find those soldiers alive. Might even be a good idea to start a party from here, backtracking to the fort."

"I'll get a posse headed out right away. What tipped you off, Wade?"

"That Army horse walking into town," Dan said. "Something about those soldiers had bothered me right from the start, but I couldn't pin it down. As far as Grover was concerned, I was a sucker for him right up to when he started shooting."

Calloway gave a low whistle. "Good thing you had your eyes open. They'd have got away with that money shipment for sure."

"More luck than anything," Dan said. "But it's all finished now."

From the deep shadows along the edge of the street Ross Oliver's harsh, threatening voice said: "Not yet, friend. Not for you."

XVI

Dan Wade wheeled about slowly. Three men were there — Oliver, Levi, and one he did not know by name. He felt his pulse quicken as the sudden press of danger again closed in upon him, then came the long, free-flowing coolness as his nerves steeled to meet the emergency.

"Out of the way, Mayor," Oliver said in that same dry tone. "You, too, storekeeper, unless you figure to use that scatter-gun."

"It's empty . . . ," Kingsford said, and bit off his words abruptly.

It would have made no difference if he had not spoken, Dan knew. Oliver was aware the gun was of no use, that its twin barrels had both been discharged, just as he could see that neither of the men carried a pistol.

"Move off," he said quietly. "No point in your mixing in this."

Calloway pulled back, quickly got out of the line of fire. Kingsford held his ground stubbornly. "I can't let you stand here alone . . . not against three of them."

"Nothing you can do about it," Dan murmured.

There was nothing anyone could do. The crowd would take no hand, would remain strictly aloof of the trouble. Kingsford said something under his breath, backed toward Calloway. Wade faced the foreman.

"You won't need them," the foreman replied evenly. "Levi and Deke won't be takin' a hand . . . not unless they have to. This here is between you and me."

"You can bet on it," Big Bill Krask's voice cut through the hush.

Wade turned his head slightly. The cattleman was on his feet. He had unpinned the town marshal's star from his son's vest and now wore it on his own. He walked slowly to Dan's side.

"That boy of mine is laying there almost dead," he said. "I've been playing a damned old fool and I reckon I'm to blame for what's happened. Now I'm getting a chance maybe to make it up to him a little."

"You hornin' in on this?" Ross Oliver asked, a definite note of pleasure in his tone.

"I am . . . if Dan here is willing."

It was the Big Bill that Wade remembered. Cold sober now, he stood, tall and wide-shouldered in that faintly stooped stance, lower jaw jutted outward, hat off, huge hands hanging at his hips.

"Welcome, friend," Dan murmured. "This is like the old days."

Krask nodded slightly. "I'll be asking your pardon, boy, when this is over. When a man takes it on to make a fool of himself, he can sure do a right fine job if he tries."

"Happens once to all of us," Dan said. He was watching Oliver and the two men. The foreman was a step or two ahead of the others. They were fanning out, each moving to the side.

"Keep your eyes peeled," Wade said, keeping his warning low. "You take Levi. I'll look after Ross and the other one."

"Fair enough," Big Bill murmured. "Watch that Ross. He's fast. We wait for them?"

"Their fight. That makes it their move."

Levi and Deke came to a sliding halt six feet on either side of the foreman. Their faces were slack, their eyes blank.

Dan said: "There's still time to call this off, Ross. No need for more killing. Throw down your guns and give

222

yourself up. You'll stand trial for your thieving and get a few years in the territory pen . . . but you'll be alive."

"The hell with you," the foreman snarled and snatched at his gun.

Dan's hand flashed down and up. He fired fast, aiming for Oliver's belly. He heard Big Bill's pistol echo his shot just as he triggered off a second at the man called Deke. Their weapons flared in unison. Dan felt the searing scorch of a bullet as it smashed into his leg, spun him half around. He lunged a step to one side, whirled back for a third shot.

There was no need. Ross Oliver lay full length in the dust. Beyond him, dead, was Levi. Deke, on his knees, clutched at his chest, a strange, drawn look on his bearded face. Suddenly he stiffened, pitched forward.

A tremor shook Dan Wade. A thick wave of sickness washed through him. He swallowed hard, took firm hold of his nerves. Death, even for the worst of men, was never a pleasant thing. It was something he could not harden himself to.

Someone broke out in a cheer. That was the release that unfettered the silent, awe-struck crowd. They surged forward in a body, gathered around Dan and Big Bill, laughing, congratulating, all striving to get close.

The rancher turned to Dan. "That apology I was mentioning, I'm making it here and now before God and everybody. I'm hoping you'll accept it and take my hand, boy."

Dan reached for the cattleman's fingers, clasped them in his own. "Forget it," he said.

"Something I won't soon be doing," Krask said.

"The marshal's going to be all right!" someone shouted from the edge of the crowd. "Doc says he's going to make it."

Dan raised his glance to the cattleman. "What about him?"

"Got some apologizing to do there, too," Big Bill said. "To him and his wife both. Maybe they'll laugh in my face when I ask them to forgive me . . . but I aim to try anyway."

"They won't laugh," Dan said. He shifted his weight. His leg, numb for several minutes, was beginning to pain.

The doctor, hatless, hair awry, pushed up to Krask's side. "They're taking the boy to my place. He'll be all right soon as I get those two bullets out of him." He turned to Dan. "Were you the one asking about Amos Kincaid?"

Wade frowned. Fear crowded into his mind again. "Yes. Is there something wrong?"

"A rancher brought him in a while ago. Found him on the road. Somebody gave him a right fierce beating. But he's all right. Amos is a tough old bird. You better come along and let me have a look at that leg."

Relief ran through Dan. "Glad to hear that," he said, adding — "I'll come in a minute." — as the physician hurried on.

"Speaking of Amos," Big Bill said. "Going to have to work myself up a new crew . . . a good one. You interested in being foreman?"

Dan Wade let his eyes drift over the

street. Volunteers were moving the dead bodies of the outlaws, of Ross Oliver and his followers. Again a slight tremor racked him. He faced the cattleman.

"I'll just take that offer," he said. "I don't think I was cut out to be a lawman."

ABOUT THE AUTHOR

Ray Hogan was an author who inspired a loyal following over the years since he published his first Western novel, *Ex-Marshal,* in 1956. Hogan was born in Willow Springs, Missouri, where his father was town marshal. When Hogan was five the family moved to Albuquerque where they lived in the foothills of the Sandia and Manzano Mountains. His father was on the Albuquerque police force and, in later years, owned the Overland Hotel. It was while listening to his father and other old-timers tell tales from the past that Ray was inspired to recast these tales in fiction. From the beginning he did exhaustive research into the history and the people of the Old West, and the walls of his study were lined with various firearms, spurs, pictures, books, and memorabilia, about all of which he could talk in dramatic detail. "I've attempted to capture the courage and bravery of those men and women that lived out West and the dangers and problems they had to overcome," Hogan once remarked. If his lawmen protagonists seem sometimes larger than life, it is because they are men of integrity, heroes who through grit of character and common sense are able to overcome the obstacles they encounter despite often overwhelming odds. This same grit of character can also be found in Hogan's heroines, and in *The Vengeance of Fortuna West* (1983) Hogan wrote a gripping and totally believable account of a woman who takes up the badge and tracks the men who killed her lawman husband by ambush. No less intriguing in her way is Nellie Dupray, convicted of rustling in *The Glory Trail* (1978). One of his most popular books, dealing with an earlier period in the West with Kit Carson as its protagonist, is *Soldier in Buckskin* (Five Star Westerns, 1996). Above all, what is most impressive about Hogan's Western novels is the consistent quality with which each is crafted, the compelling depth of his characters, and his ability to juxtapose the complexities of human conflict into narratives always as intensely interesting as they are emotionally involving.